GOING DOWN

the INSTINCT guide to oral sex

BEN R. ROGERS & JOEL PERRY

illustrations by DAVID L. KELLY

Acknowledgments

Ben and Joel would like to thank the following people:

Everyone who has ever given us a blow job, good or bad—you're in here.
Our parents for paying for college so we could write a book about cock sucking.
The professional sex workers of America.
Fred for putting up with Joel.
Ben's other personalities for putting up with Ben.
The staff at *Instinct* for putting up with Ben.
The entire Los Angeles basin for putting *out* for Ben.
All the people who so generously shared their experiences with us, especially those in the porno section at the local video store.
And to Dan Cullinane at Alyson, who gave us the opportunity to be able to say, for the rest of our lives, "Don't give me any shit, I wrote the book on blow jobs!"

* The percentages scattered throughout the book were gathered from an online survey *Instinct* conducted. There were 645 respondents.

MANUFACTURED IN THE UNITED STATES OF AMERICA.

THIS TRADE PAPERBACK ORIGINAL IS PUBLISHED BY ALYSON PUBLICATIONS,
P.O. BOX 4371, LOS ANGELES, CALIFORNIA 90078-4371.
DISTRIBUTION IN THE UNITED KINGDOM BY TURNAROUND PUBLISHER SERVICES LTD.,
UNIT 3, OLYMPIA TRADING ESTATE, COBURG ROAD, WOOD GREEN,
LONDON N22 6TZ ENGLAND.

FIRST EDITION: MAY 2002

02 03 04 05 06 **a** 10 9 8 7 6 5 4 3 2

ISBN 1-55583-752-2

COVER PHOTOGRAPHY BY KEVIN BAILEY.

Contents

Introduction: The Meaning of Life   1

1: What's Not to Love?   7

2: You Don't Know Dick   21

3: Hot Spots   37

4: Head of the Class   47

5: Blow His Mind   61

6: Operation Deep-Throat   79

7: Pole Positions   89

8: The Best I Ever Had   97

9: Location, Location, Location   111

10: Let's Finish This Off   133

introduction
THE MEANING OF LIFE

OK, we lied. Sorta. This little instruction manual isn't going to explain your existence. Nor is it going to teach you how to be a better person, save the rain forests, or help you cook a meal without using a microwave. It can, however, help you learn to suck your partner's dick like he'd like it to be sucked. And isn't that what we're all here on Earth for? To help each other? To give one another a little pleasure so long as it doesn't hurt anyone else or interfere with Must See TV? Congratulations on picking up this book! It means you want to make the world a better place!

Whatever. The real reason we cut down all those trees to print this puppy is because we were tired of hearing about all you boys and girls giving bad head. Hell, we even came across some of you freaks who don't even like licking your man's private popsicle AT ALL. Once the shock wore off (two months and many margaritas later), we realized that our once simple mission to bring better blow jobs to the masses was going to be a lot more difficult than we'd planned.

Now, if you're already pretty darned good at fellating your fella, please accept a great big wet thank-you from us. We love you. Especially since you're looking at this book with a desire to improve your skills and get even better at it. (Either that, or you're thinking about giving it to someone who should. That works too.) But there are some people out there who are not as evolved as you, and we need to address their sorry asses also.

See, we are of the esteemed opinion that sex, in general, is one of the greatest evolutionary advances ever. Or, if you're of the religious mind-set, one of God's grandest creations. Or, for you existentialists waiting around for your imminent, meaningless demise into empty, black nothingness, it's a great way to pass the time. However you choose to look at it, we all do it, so why do it badly?

Oral sex, in particular, seems to be one area in which a lot of people come up lacking. A good majority of the people we kidnapped, tied up, and interrogated for this book seemed to agree that there's a lot of tension surrounding giving a man a little mouth-to-cock. For something that's supposed to be so stress-relieving, there are still a lot of uptight people walking around, partly because they either can't get a decent hummer at home or because it's Thursday and they know what their main squeeze is going to be expecting after his favorite show. In other words, there are too many of you losers…er, we mean, *otherwise decent human beings* who either suck at sucking or have made up some lame excuse in your mind why you can't (or won't) baste your man's ham.

Since you're probably not reading this book on a plane or in some coffee shop (and if you are, more power to ya), let's be honest, OK? When was the last time you asked a friend if he or she enjoys giving head and had them respond with, "Sure, I guess it's OK?" Rarely, if ever, huh? Bring up oral sex and the men and women going south have firm ideas about what they like and dislike; there are hardly any middle-of-the-road opinions about feasting on your man's beast. (Oh, and if you're tired of the euphemisms already, not to mention the offhand tone, get over it. Having a sense of humor about the experience, no matter how silly, can actually make it all the more enjoyable!) When it comes to sucking dick, either you can't get enough or you'd rather have your eyelashes pulled out one by one. There are going to be exceptions, of course, but most gay men and straight women see it as a black-or-white issue.

You'd think that with sexual liberation would come a desire to go out and try everything, even if it is just for one night. Yet even something as basic as a blow job has become a complex issue. On the surface, it seems like all you have to do is stick it in your mouth, bob up and down a few times, and decide whether to spit or swallow. Well, then you start to factor in timing, hygiene, the guy's size, how long he lasts, paying attention to other parts of his body, sore jaw muscles, getting pubes stuck in your teeth, and WHAM! it seems like so much work for something that's supposed to be exciting and pleasurable.

However, this doesn't have to be the case. In fact, we're firm believers in the joys of giving and getting head. Hell, we should be out doing it right now instead of sitting here writing a book about it. There's a strong conviction around *Instinct* magazine that if guys started getting better quality blows from their partners, we'd have a lot more happy campers and fewer assholes on the freeway cutting us off. Hmm, maybe we really *are* just trying to make the world a better place.

Now, usually in these intros the author (or authors) make some comments about the title of the book, and why they were inspired to write it, and give a brief summary of what you, the dear reader, is hopefully going to be taking away from the whole experience, blah blah blah. Well, the title pretty much explains itself: We've already told you about our inspiring inspiration for penning this guide, and you're going to put this book down in a few hours and go give your partner the best blow job of his life. Can Virginia Woolf, Ernest Hemingway, Tennessee Williams, and Stephen Hawking claim that? Didn't think so.

Basically, what all our rambling is about is that oral sex is an important part of most people's sexual lives. If you are dating a male of the human species, it's a good bet that he likes to get his dick sucked. What's more, since you're the one lying next to him in bed, he would probably really dig it if you were the one slobbering on his knob.

But here's the catch, and it may come off as a subtle threat: When you won't do it, he may find someone who will. Don't believe us? Five words: prostitutes and public rest rooms. If you're planning on loving him long time, it's in your best interest to love all of him, as often as you can, and with as many creative twists and turns as you can muster. But if the possibility of being kicked to the curb isn't reason enough to change your attitude or fine-tune your blow job techniques, we'll give you another: reputation. If your teeth scraped up your last date's dick or if you puked all over his crotch, word is going to get around. No man is going to want to touch you. Ever. (Scared now? Good. We figured that with all the religious creeps and misinformation about STDs keeping some of us from humping like rabbits, we'd climb on that ugly bandwagon to freak you back into gettin' it on and gettin' it right.)

Maybe it's a tad dramatic to assume that he'll ditch you if you're not servicing him as much as he'd like, but we've heard of guys hitting the road for much less. (Of course, we may just be hanging out with the wrong people.) The point is, though, that men are pretty simple to please. It's true. They need (1) some sleep, (2) to have their egos stroked every so often, (3) a few meals throughout the day, and (4) frequent sex. Most will even give up the food and shut-eye for more sex. But if these basic needs aren't met, well, you know the rest.

And even if you're one of those guys or gals we mentioned above who can't wait to get on your knees, it's highly likely that you and your man aren't getting all you can from oral sex. This book will inspire a lot of you to strive to be even better. Sure, there are those of you who make Patsy from *Absolutely Fabulous* look like a nun. Well, maybe you'll learn that there's a lot more involved than how well you suppress your gag reflex or how long you are able to hold your breath. Then again, you may just be a big slut who has forgotten what it's like to breathe through your mouth.

Finally, while there is a lot of info contained between these covers, the main thing you should take from the stories, advice, and cute little illustrations is that going down IS fun. It shouldn't be a chore or something your partner has to beg for (although that might be a kinky twist). So commit these pages to memory, rip off his pants, and take him where nobody has taken him before.

Just watch the teeth, OK?

1
WHAT'S NOT TO LOVE?

We guessed that the best way to prepare before you find yourself on your knees going where only a few dozen (or is it a few hundred?) people have gone before is to brush all your worries away. That's it. Relax. Take a deep breath, close your eyes, and imagine yourself in a lush tropical paradise far away from any cell phones, road rage, or boy bands. Can't you see yourself lying on a secluded beach without a worry in the world, the only appointment you have being your 1:30 with a muscular masseur back at the hotel villa? Ahhh. Doesn't that sound nice? WELL, SNAP OUT OF IT! You just shelled out a few bucks for this book, which is hardly enough to cover the airplane food on the trip to said tropical destination, so you're just gonna have to settle for the cheap way to handle problems (and, no, we don't mean Ben & Jerry's).

GAY-STRAIGHT ALLIANCE

Now you've heard the popular saying (and maybe read the popular book) "Men are from Mars, women are from Venus"? Well, when it comes to oral sex, this adage proves to be a bunch of malarkey. Maybe not *complete* bullshit—there are a *few* things that gay men and straight women don't see eye-to-eye on when they head south—but you might be surprised at how much agreement there is between the sexes about BJs. Come on, a penis is a penis, so you'd expect the reactions to sucking and licking and nibbling on one to be pretty much the same, correct?

That's right. Even though gay men are also affectionately known as cocksuckers, that doesn't mean that they *all* turn into vacuums at the sight of an exposed prick *or* that they pop outta their momma knowing how to please every man on the planet. Far from it. (In fact, we have a list going of homos we'd like to "give back" to the straight world; they're no use to us, being lousy in bed.) And it's not like all breeder boys aren't getting proper lovin' from their girlfriends. There are a respectable number of women who can give Samantha on *Sex and the City* a run for her money.

However, fags have the same equipment, so that instantly puts them on a more level playing field with whomever they choose to play. Sure, there may be discrepancies in size and shape, but a man already knows what feels good to him, and it's likely that the same (or similar) things feel good for his partner. What can we say except, hey, it's a guy thing? As you read on about the concerns both men and women have, you'll notice that boys aren't really as hung up on the physical aspects as girls are. Like we said, how can you be turned off by a dick when you have one yourself? (Ask any hetero guy this question and watch him get stumped.) Aside from that, both sexes pretty much complain about the same things.

Yes, complain. We know, we know: *At least they're getting some,* you're thinking. How can they be finding fault when there are mil-

54%

of men say they never have to be coaxed into giving a blow job.

lions of men and women out there right now starving to have somebody even look their way? Well, unlike *some* people, these weenie-loving whiners decided to actually chat about why they don't polish their man's power tool more often. See, the whole point of this chapter is to get the baggage out of the way: to talk about all the "issues" so everything that follows reads like you're part of some cocksucking carnival. The people that get to ride the most are the ones that talk about what they enjoy and what they can't stand. It's called communication. You know, some of you majored in it during college and realized that, after five years, you were now qualified to put files in alphabetical order? Perhaps that degree isn't so worthless after all.

Before we continue, though, let's get something straight right now. There are valid concerns, and then there's you being a picky little bitch. Him grabbing your head when you don't want him to or not trimming his pubes so you'd need a machete to find his lost treasure—those are valid concerns you'll want to address. That you kicked him out because his dick was only 7.92 inches instead of the eight he promised at the bar, or that you think spending 15 minutes between his thighs means you're married—these are what we'll call obnoxious reactions. For obvious reasons, we're only going to cover the serious hurdles we encountered and hope all you petty people get some help. Soon. Let's get started…

WHOSE TURN IS IT, ANYWAY?

"Giving head is great, don't get me wrong," asserted Daniel, 32. "What sucks is when I get him home only to find out that this is going to be a one-sided hookup. If I'm going to work my magic on a guy, I feel he should do the same. I'm happy giving him pleasure, but that only goes so far. If he comes and isn't into finishing me off, or if he wants to just lay back and do nothing, I won't have it. He's gone."

Daniel has, thankfully, only had to boot a few guys, but he brings up a good point, one that both men *and* women on the giving end confront on a regular basis: One-sided sex doesn't work. Let's play a little game, shall we? First, you have to be in an unaroused state, so stop fiddling with yourself, and think about Rosie O'Donnell—naked. Now think about some of the things you do during sex but from a clinical perspective. Would a rational person, say, rim another person? You know, dive between the butt cheeks with their tongue?

No. But a lot of you enjoy doing it when the lights go out and everybody is in the buff. Why? Because when all that blood rushes from your brain and floods your groin it's not about being rational, it's about what feels good. You stick your finger up your boyfriend's butt because it drives him wild, not because you're performing a prostate exam (well, at least not one they teach you at med school). Same thing goes for oral sex. You're not down there licking his stick for science, buddy; You're doing it because it's pleasurable, for him *and* you.

When Daniel meets these bozos who could care less what he likes, he's totally in the right to show them the door. True, you'll stumble upon fellas or ladies along the way who wouldn't even think of asking you to reciprocate, but either they have major self-esteem issues or, surprise surprise, they get their rocks off getting *your* rocks off.

Of course, we're not going to completely slam the bastards who think they can lay back, throw their arms behind their heads, let poor little you do all the work, and then pass out thinking they're the ones that accomplished something. (Seriously, who do these guys think they are? Republicans?) Instead, we tracked one of these moochers down, got him to admit his bad behavior, and then asked him how the hell he gets away with it.

"You can get away with a lot of things for one night," said Terence, one of many (too many, if you ask us) mid-20s "personal assistants" in Los Angeles. "Besides, if you're going home with somebody the night you meet, it's obviously for sex. If you know you're not going to get into a relationship, then you don't really need to run all the bases, right?" He added, "I don't really like giving head to somebody whose last name I don't even know, much less go all the way. If he wants to suck me off, great. But I don't feel I should have to do the same."

Both Terence's and Daniel's arguments point to a few of the perils of fly-by-night fucking. First, Terence is right: If you go home with some stranger and vaguely remember that his name starts with an *M* (or is it *N*?), it's most likely because you two want to play Doctor. Does the sex really mean that much? Probably not, unless it's your first time or if you haven't gotten laid since grunge was popular. However, Daniel is also correct in his assertion, provided that he talks to his partners beforehand and lets them know that he wants it to be mutual. Just throw it into the conversation. "So, what do you do? Would you like another drink? If I take you home and suck you dry, will you do the same for me?"

56% of women say they feel that they give their partners enough oral sex.

The key to making this work is simple. Daniel goes over and hits on Terence. After some friendly chitchat, Daniel asks Terence to come back to his place and works in that he likes to give and receive. Terence says he only likes to receive. Daniel tells him good luck and is privately thankful he didn't buy Terence a drink. They both move on to somebody else.

There you have it. In order to avoid taking somebody home who isn't going to make you tingle, you'll need to talk to him. That's right, girls and boys! It's all about com-mun-i-ca-tion. Even if forming sentences isn't your forte, after a few basic questions you can discover if tonight's conquest is going to be worth your time. If not, there is a sea of men out there waiting to be plundered by your marvelous self.

OH, HOW THE YEARS BLOW BY

To many people, though, sex is more enjoyable in the confines of a relationship. When you've moved past the nights of not knowing (or really caring about) what his last name is, the doors suddenly open to a whole new world of intimacy. Not necessarily "Oprah intimacy," where you two constantly babble about your feelings like lesbians, but rather a higher comfort level—especially with your bodies. Yet feeling content is a double-edged sword. On one side you two know each other's likes and dislikes; on the other, knowing what to expect takes away some of the thrill you got when you were single and brought a new boy toy home every weekend. It's like a present when you were a little kid: You were all excited to play with it on your birthday, but six months later it's in a box to be donated to charity. Then again, a guy's dick is probably more fun to play with than Legos. (OK, calm down! We did say *probably*. Sheesh.)

Before you get all depressed and go overdose on Tylenol, we'd like to inform you that coupling up doesn't have to mean the death of sex. Really. Stop laughing! So what if you two don't have sex eight times a week anymore? Ever hear of quality over quantity? Think about those "studs" who run around town in their tight clothes and overly insured cars. Let's say they get together with two guys or gals per week. Now, if one out of every eight of them can pull off a decent dick sucking, congratulations: The stud was only satisfied one time this month. If you and your partner have a quality romp once a week, you are still four times more satisfied than the horndog that everybody's after. Don't you just love math? (However, if all those guys and girls read this book and perfect their techniques, you and your hubby are gonna have to bump it up a notch to keep the players in their place. Are you, heh heh, *up* to the challenge?)

Jack and Jill (we know it's disgusting, but those *are* their names) have been together for 12 years. They've seen three presidents in office, sent their first E-mails to each other, and have almost broken up over the wild thing (or lack of it) about as often as Madonna changes her persona. "We love each other," Jill assures us, "but Jack is much more sexual than I am. It seems like he wants it every day, while I'm content with maybe once or twice per week." (Hmm, a guy who wants some more than a girl. That's a novel idea.)

On the surface, it appears that our het couple should just add up how many times they'd like to have sex and divide it in half. Easy enough compromise, correct? Actually, no. Even if they agreed to this method, Jack would come up short of what he wants (although he'd be bumpin' uglies more often than previously) and Jill's heart probably wouldn't be into it every time. We know what all you jaded single types are thinking at this moment: *Jill should allow Jack to get some booty on the side.* However, that isn't what these two want, so you can go spread your hedonistic influences elsewhere. Jack and Jill need another solution.

What? You think *we're* going to provide one? Oh, all right, as long as it gets you off our backs. Let's go back to the whole "quality over quantity" argument. Jill can still keep her two times a week, but she's going to have to make up those five missing days to Jack when they make love, sweet love. And if you were starting to think that we were veering away from blow jobs for a little bit there, here's how they fit in for J & J. Jill admitted that she usually gets right to the "main event," which for them is missionary. (Oh, sorry, was that us yawning?) What our happy couple needs to focus on then is varying their sexual repertoire. Reintroducing oral sex into their bedtime stories is a start. For Jill, learning about how many ways she can blow her man's mind (literally and figuratively) is the rest of the race. Making a whole night out of playing "Suck, Suck, Goose!" is one way of crossing the finish line. Of course, as we saw in the previous section, Jack is gonna have to return the favor—but unfortunately, that form of reciprocation is another book. (All you gay boys can stop squirming now.)

GIVE IT TO ME, BABY!

We're pretty sure that when you told him to "give it" to you, you meant however many inches he's sporting—and not some nasty STD. Concern over disease transmittal is ostensibly something else that pops up when you're going down. Yes, it is kind of weird to slap a condom on his cock when giving him head. It's like giving a noogie to someone wearing a helmet. What's more, they have yet to invent dick-flavored condoms, and concealing your love gun can take away from the more subtle sensations of oral pleasure. Plus, they never cover up during the hummer scenes in any of the porns we've watched, and those people have had sex with *way* more people than you, right? Right?

13

It may come as a shock to some of ya, but porn isn't exactly indicative of completely healthy sexual behavior. They're trying to turn on their viewers, which doesn't quite work if the star of the show is covered up the whole time. Anyway, those of you (and be aware that this is mostly men we're talking about right now) who take all your sexual cues from porn probably are the same guys who can't imagine a sexual encounter that doesn't involve cheap dirty talk and simultaneous orgasms. Back in the real world it's important to remember that sex of any kind is never 100% foolproof.

Take HIV, for example. Some studies have shown that, over time, 1% to 7% of people who contract HIV do so through unprotected oral sex. Of course, even these numbers are considered high throughout the medical community. There are also quite a few doctors who have professed that they are unable to make a connection between dick sucking and HIV contraction. Most researchers point out how hard it is to separate the different kinds of sex people can have (anal, vaginal, and oral) to actually determine which one spreads the virus.

10% of people make a blow job the main event during their sex play.

However, most studies show that the risk of walking away with anything other than another date are small—*much* more minute than anal or vaginal intercourse. Yet there is still a risk we have to tell you about because we don't want to get sued—er, we mean because we love you. We know that, if your partner is positive, his come contains HIV. But so does his precome, so stopping before he shoots doesn't mean you're home free. Nor does not brushing your teeth, as many of you seem to think. Although saliva and stomach acids are hardly HIV's best friends, even if you don't brush and floss before a hot date, there are still small openings in your mouth that HIV can pass through. Same thing goes for a host of other nasty critters. Gonorrhea, HPV, herpes, and hepatitis, just to mention a few, can all be transmitted during oral sex. You should consult your doctor or local health clinic for further info about the risks of having unprotected oral sex.

That we have to bring all this up is a bummer, we know. Alas, there are steps you can take to put your mind at ease. One is to wrap yourself in plastic, lock yourself in a bomb shelter, and never come in contact with another human being again. However, the thought of never having sex again is probably making some of you sweat right now, so we'll toss that suggestion in the garbage.

The easiest option is to put a lid on lover boy's come cannon. A condom, even if it only covers the head, can greatly reduce the chance of any of his juices getting in your mouth. That still allows for you to lick up and down the shaft, tongue his balls, and do loads of other wicked things to various parts of his body to make up for the slightly reduced sensation he's experiencing from having his supersensitive head covered up. There are even flavored condoms to make the experience more enjoyable for the suckers. (You should avoid condoms and lube that use nonoxynol-9, especially during anal and oral intercourse. This spermicide can numb and irritate the inside of your mouth, making you more susceptible to HIV transmission.)

Even better is for both of you to get screened for STDs. If either one (or both) of you find out you have something, it's OK: The doctor can provide some helpful advice on how you two can still go about doing the wild thing. The worst thing you two can do is—TA DA!—*not* talk about it. As with most dilemmas that aren't discussed, it can only make it worse.

WORKIN' HARD FOR YOUR HONEY

You're probably aware that sex is, hands down, probably the best reason to sweat. You can burn a decent number of calories during nookie (about 150 every 15 minutes), so if you can't make it to the gym, well, you have a solid reason to stay in bed on Sunday. But what about those of you who feel you're getting burned burning all those calories? A handful of the people we liquored up confessed that they feel there's too much work involved during oral sex. Again, we couldn't figure out exactly how they came to this conclusion, so we bought another round and tried to view the world through these lazy asses' eyes.

Jeff, a 29-year-old engineer, sure acts like he gets enough from his boyfriend of two years, but he admitted that it's mostly "standard sex" in his bedroom. "I used to love giving and getting head a few years back, but back then gay sex was new to me. I feel like I grew out of blow jobs."

Yes, he graduated from blow jobs and fun sex to…predictable shags. That's not what we'd call growing up. It's more like growing bored. Now, we'd just slap Jeff around for a bit and send him on his way if he complained about being too old to enjoy sex like he used to, but he said that it was a feeling he couldn't shake (plus he's kind of hot), so we decided to probe a little deeper. (Into his *problem*, thanks.)

We could easily say that, similar to Jack and Jill, Jeff had grown accustomed to his routine. However, Jack and Jill have been together six times longer than Jeff and his boyfriend, so we're not going to let him off the hook that easily.

Instead, here's where you start to ask some rather revealing questions regarding your relationship. We've already beat communication to death, so we'll assume you got our point about that. (And if you didn't, we'll find you sooner or later.) Two years into a relationship, eh? That's an important milestone. Maybe it's time Jeff started asking himself whether he's sure about the guy. Hypothetically speaking, if they broke up and Jeff met someone new, would he start enjoying going down more? Two years isn't a great amount of time for a couple's sex life to descend into being "standard," is it? You know, maybe it is. That's right, having a completely predictable romp is what most

67% of men allow their partners to come in their mouths.

of us want. Screw pushing our limits or discovering that being tied up is fun. Or that role-playing can add new dimensions of intimacy. Or that pumping your man dry like an oil company in Alaska can be the main event for the evening.

All right, we'll stop with the sarcasm for a little bit. It's just hard to not be facetious when we hear people consider draining their man's hose a chore. People, people, people—we were able to write an *entire* book about blow jobs. They've fit the histories of small countries into fewer pages. Right about now you should be figuring out that hummers are a lot more than a sexual act you perform because you're too tired to get completely undressed. There is so much to write about, not because it's complicated per se but rather because, simply put, there's so much fun you can make from three simple ingredients: his wang, your mouth, and no prior commitments.

Sarah, a 34-year-old lawyer out of San Francisco, found herself in a situation similar to Jeff's. "I recently got out of a five-year relationship," she said. "And while we hardly broke up because he wasn't getting enough head from me, I look back and see that oral sex was pretty much nonexistent during the last year. It was something I did because I loved him and he enjoyed it, but once our relationship started to die down, so did everything but the quickies we had once a week before we went to work."

It may be the time to start wondering about where you're headed in your relationship, because while it could be something small, sex is also a great indicator of larger issues. We hate to refer back to this book that you're reading again, but if you are in a romp rut, why the hell did you pick this fine piece of literature up if you didn't think there was more potential to sex—especially the oral kind? Just something to think about. Next topic!

"EW, WHAT IN GOD'S NAME IS THAT?"

Some people may be uncomfortable with the male body because it's a bit mysterious to them. Not everybody humps with the lights on, you know? And even if you regularly fuck under the glare of the stadium lights at Fenway Park, you may have never taken the opportunity to explore your hairy friend fully. Yet as you've probably guessed, this is more of an issue between hetero couples. (Those troublemakers!)

You may find giving head unappealing because when it comes to fucking so much of the focus is on the penis. Granted, a lot of this has to do with basic male mentality, but even we'll admit that, taken as a separate limb, a lot of pricks look suspiciously similar to one of the creatures we saw in *Aliens*. We don't know about you, but acid-spewing monsters don't really do anything for us in the hormone department. You sometimes forget about his cute little butt that you noticed when you first met him or that he used his hunky biceps to throw you in bed in the first place. OK, so we spend the entire next chapter just discussing his love log, but we *are* talking about blow jobs. Besides, chapter 3 is about everything else you can poke and prod and twist on his body to make the experience orgasmic.

As a primer, we suggest that next time you're engaged in a sexual encounter that lasts longer than the time it takes the security guard to make his bathroom rounds, do some Lewis and Clarking of your own. Tell him to lie back and relax. Trust us, he won't resist. If he's good enough to co-sign on the mortgage, he damn better well be worth it to touch all over. Check out his nipples. See how the scrotum feels in your hand and how the testicles move around inside. Brush over his body hair. He'll probably get aroused and try to grope you, but just slap him away and flip him over for the rear view. The point to this particular exercise is not to please him, really, but to please you. (And if this isn't pleasing to you, shouldn't you be wondering why you're in bed naked next to him?)

Above all, don't fret about exploring his body. Firstly, the gentle touching will soothe and stimulate him. Secondly, if you throw out the occasional "Oh, that's nice" or "Mmm, this is hot," he'll dig the admiration. Really, never underestimate the male ego.

ON YOUR KNEES!

While some sexpot barking orders at us like an army captain can make us stiff in the blink of an eye, we're aware that there are a lot of you who consider giving head as something demeaning. True, you're on your knees and can't really talk (with your mouth full and all). But here's something to ponder: If the guy is such a friggin' tyrant, why don't you just bite it off and be done with it? In other words, you're pretty much in control, no matter how regal he thinks he looks.

When both of you approach this as respectful equals (which you are) with an attitude of fun and pleasure (which you should have), where is the demeaning element? Here's a hint: There ain't one. If you're the sucker (and we mean that in a completely affirmative way, dudes and dudettes), it's your choice who gets the honor of your blow job, right? If the guy is an asshole, don't suck his cock. Is this a difficult concept to grasp? If there is more than one beau vying for your attention, you get to choose the nicest or richest or most hung one, don'tcha? Let us repeat: He wants you to butter his corncob really, really badly. You hold the cards. Tired of him bad-mouthing your mother? He'll zip those lips. Want him to scrub the toilet? Wash your car? Consider it done with the promise of a good cock sucking.

Oh, and before you go and get your panties in a wad, princess, we are NOT advocating withholding sex as healthy relationship behavior. That's not good for anyone. We know, because our parents did it to each other, took it out on us, and now we're buying our therapists very expensive cars.

What we are saying is that your ability to suck him like Robert Downey Jr. sucking up cocaine is a powerful thing, and it should make you feel powerful. Taking his most valuable player into your mouth is not an act of submission (unless you're into that scene), or weakness, or humiliation. It's a brilliant way of giving pleasure to another person.

Well, enough of this cheerleading crap. Let's get down to business!

2

YOU DON'T KNOW DICK

Or maybe you do. But then you wouldn't be reading this book if you didn't already *love* dick, so you won't mind looking at one in detail. We'll start with a road map to the little monster, but start taking some mental notes—there's a quiz at the end!

I AM JOE'S COCK

The dick actually begins a few inches inside the body at the "root," where the spongy erectile tissue starts just under the pubic bone. Oh, and while we're on the subject of bones, despite the term *boner*, there is no bone in the human dick. Neither is it a muscle, so we don't care if he does call it his "muscle of love." There are, however, two lovely little suspensory ligaments that go from the pubic bone to the base of the penis. You know when the guy makes his erect cock jerk upward with a bounce? He's using those ligaments.

When a guy gets an operation to make his dick longer, cutting those ligaments is the first thing the doc does. That makes them release their "hold" on man's real best friend, so a little more of your tadger falls out of the body, making it appear longer. Congratulations, you've now got from one to two more inches of meat, but bye-bye bounce. Oh, and it'll hang down, even when hard. And one more thing: That gain is only while soft. When erect, the gain is usually much less than an inch, so you're now more of a shower than a grow-er.

MAKING IT BIG, STARTING WITH THE...

Shaft! He's a bad mother—(shut your mouth)! I'm just talkin' about the shaft—the length of man meat that sticks out of the body, down (or up, as the case may be) to the head. The shaft is composed mostly of spongy erectile tissue called corpus cavernosum—that's for you geeks, but don't get too excited, because we're never going to use that term again. That tissue is wrapped in a rigid sheath called the tunica albuginea. Fancy words, we know, but it's this simple: When your man is watching the news, his penis hangs limp because that spongy tissue isn't filled with blood (unless he has a thing for Stone Phillips or Cokie Roberts). The blood is going in and then right back out again in a normal fashion. When your man is watching porn—or you doing that thing with the cucumber—he gets all excited and turned on. The muscles around the blood vessels leading into his schlong relax, letting more blood in, and the muscles around the vessels that lead away constrict. The blood starts to collect, creating pressure that fills the spongy tissue, which presses hard against the rigid sheath, *et viola,* hard-on! When he's hard, you can probe gently but firmly just behind his balls, where you'll feel the root or bulb of his penis. Press it and you'll note a quick, temporary swell in his dick. Actually, that's a rather pleasant sensation, so file that away for use in your sexual repertoire.

Typically after ejaculation, or when he gets tired of you, those blood vessels return to normal and the excess blood can leave the penis in an orderly and organized manner. He goes limp again. Then there follows awhile before his soldier can stand at full attention. This is called a refractory period. It's different for each dude, but if you're wanting to go at it again, you're gonna need to let some time pass. No need to call a halt to lovemaking, though. There are plenty of other things he can be doing to you in the

50% of people prefer to suck on an average-size penis during oral sex.

meantime. And if you haven't finished and he's *not* doing any of those things, seriously reconsider who you'll be seeing next Saturday night. But back to boners and what makes them work.

BASIC PLUMBING

The urethra also travels down the length of the shaft on the underside. That's what carries urine from the bladder, past the prostate, and out of the body through the penis. The reason you want to know about the urethra is because, once you've learned everything in this fine instruction manual about sucking your partner off good, it's also gonna be carrying all that semen you're sucking outta your studmuffin. Part of the urethra is surrounded by ringlike muscles (the ischiocavernosus muscles) that contract in sequence during orgasm. This progressive wave of contraction and relaxation is called peristalsis,

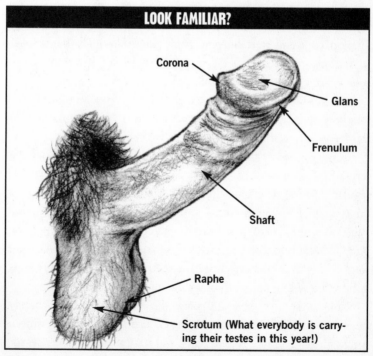

LOOK FAMILIAR?

Corona

Glans

Frenulum

Shaft

Raphe

Scrotum (What everybody is carrying their testes in this year!)

and it's what pushes the jizz out in spurts. You've heard of shooting a load? That's how it gets shot. The urethra ends at the tip of the penis at what professionals call the urethral opening—and what we Regular Joes romantically refer to as the piss slit.

IT'S ALL COMING TO A HEAD

At the end of the penis is the head. It's the part that looks like a German World War II helmet. Where it flares out around the head (the "brim" of the helmet) is called the corona. That's where the foreskin (or prepuce) is attached on an uncircumcised penis. Conversely, it's where the foreskin was removed on a circumcised dick. The foreskin, if intact, is the skin that covers the head of the penis. The head has the most nerve endings, so you'll be paying particular attention to this part once we finally pucker up and go down. All those nerve endings have been protected by the foreskin on an uncircumcised cock, so you can expect them to be re-e-eally sensitive. Use that to your advantage. Pull that foreskin back and start slurping away, baby! Although the exposed nerves aren't quite as near the surface on the head of a circumcised cock, it's still plenty sensitive and ready for play.

Foreskin protects the head of the penis by acting as a hood over this very sensitive part. Most American men (an estimated two thirds) are circumcised, having had this skin chopped off at infancy. A creamy or cheesy substance called smegma can form under the foreskin of an unwashed penis, but it can be prevented easily with regular cleaning. There are those who like a little dick cheese. Many do not. It's up to you to voice—and act on—your opinion. Whether you find it unpleasant or deliciously masculine, we're not here to be judgmental but to give you the facts. Whatever kind of foreskin you want (i.e., with or without cheese), let him know, because the point is to have fun with it and both of you to enjoy yourselves.

Sometimes guys who still have their foreskin find it handy because it's a movable sheath over the dick and needs no lubrication. An uncut guy can just grab his cock and start whacking away. As for those of us who are cut, well, that's why God made lube and spit. At any rate, it's not going to affect things very much one way or the other when it comes to giving head, so don't worry your pretty little, uh, head.

Where were we? Oh, yeah, that lovely rounded part from the corona to the piss slit—I mean urethral opening—is called the glans. You'll be licking that a lot. (*Glans* is Latin for "acorn," for those of you going on *Jeopardy!*) Just below the piss slit on the underside of the

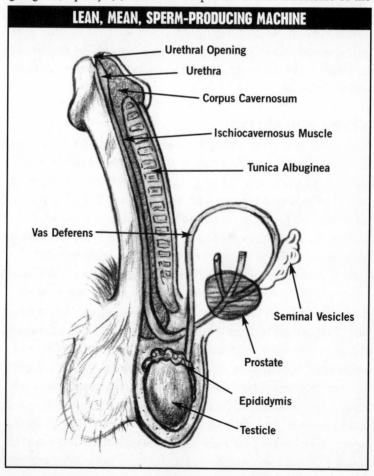

LEAN, MEAN, SPERM-PRODUCING MACHINE

Urethral Opening
Urethra
Corpus Cavernosum
Ischiocavernosus Muscle
Tunica Albuginea
Vas Deferens
Seminal Vesicles
Prostate
Epididymis
Testicle

59%

of people consider genital piercings a turnoff.

head at its base is a little Y-shaped membrane, the frenulum (also known as the frenum, Alex). It's another point where the foreskin is connected to the shaft, and it can be quite sensitive to sexual stimulation, whether your man is cut or uncut.

It is also perfectly normal for a penis to curve up, down, or to either side. During the dirty deed you'll want to experiment with positioning yourself so that curve naturally finds its way down your throat. But we're getting ahead of ourselves. Dicks can also twist in any number of directions and even be straight as an arrow. It's all part of nature's wonderful variety.

HAVING A BALL—OR TWO

Now we need to stray a little from Mr. Superstar and meet some very important supporting players: the balls, the nads, the family jewels—*en Español:* the *huevos,* or *cojones.* The testicles hang down below the dick in a sac (not *sack,* thank you) called the scrotum. Why? Because for these puppies to manufacture sperm—which is, after all, their *job*—they need to be 2 to 4 degrees Fahrenheit below body temperature. Swinging down there in the scrotum outside the body is kinda like an air conditioning system. Make that a self-regulating AC system, because that's what's going on when the balls move up and down inside the scrotum, depending on the temperature. That also explains the "shrinkage" that occurs when a man gets out of a chilly pool. Cold makes 'em scurry back up into the nice, warm body. If a guy wants low-hangers, he should hang in a sauna. But not too long. Maintaining a constant high temperature will affect sperm production. That's why close-fitting tighty whities that jam his nuts up into his body can, over time, lower a guy's sperm count, so make sure your man buys a size up if that's important to you. We should also mention that it's perfectly normal for one ball to hang lower than the other, so don't go freaking out over that.

You may notice a line or ridge that starts under the penis and divides the scrotum in two, one testicle on each side. That's sort of a seam from when the genitals were forming in the womb, and it's called a raphe (ray'-fee). Bet it's one of those things you never knew had a name, huh? Like that place under your nose called the, uh, the…thingummy. (Hmm, guess we should stick to dick.) Anyway, the raphe on some men also continues all the way back to the anus, and the main reason we brought it up at all was: (1) to show you we really do research these things; (2) to teach you stuff you can use in cocktail conversations ("Oh, really, Ted? Well, bite my raphe!" Or "When your balls get cold and your scrotum shrivels up, have you noticed how squiggly your raphe becomes, rabbi?"); and (3) to point out something that, when you're at a loss for what to do next, you can always tickle with your tongue. But let's get back to the twins.

Now then, the testicles are

JIZZ THE FACTS, MA'AM!

Average age at which a man starts sperm production: 12.5 years

Average amount of semen per ejaculation: 1–2 teaspoons, or 2–5 cc's

Average number of sperm per ejaculate: 280 million

Population of the United States: Approximately 280 million

Percent of semen made up of sperm: 5%

Number of calories per teaspoon of semen: 7 (So low! Have more!)

Average total lifetime ejaculate: Approximately 14 gallons

Average speed of ejaculation: 23–28 m.p.h. (Ow, my eye!)

Sperm life, from development to ejaculation: 2.5 months

Estimated number of times a man will ejaculate in his life: 7,200

Of those, the estimated percent from masturbation: 28% (Which seems suspiciously low, but then that could just be us)

Content of semen: Ascorbic acid, blood-group antigens, calcium, cholesterol, choline, citric acid, creatine, DNA, fructose glutathione, hyaluronidase, lactic acid, magnesium, nitrogen, phosphorus, potassium, purine, pyrimidine, pyruvic acid, sodium, sorbitol, spermidine, spermine, urea, uric acid, vitamin B-12 and zinc tender little guys, so you don't want to go banging around down there indiscriminately. When a man doubles over because somebody tagged his jewels, it's not an exaggeration and it's no joke. If the nads are hurting, there will be no sex tonight. So yes, they are somewhat delicate, but that also makes them extremely sensitive to sexual stimulation, so be prepared to nuzzle up to that scrotum. The amount of stimulation the balls are able to take varies greatly from man to man. Some guy's nuts are so tender you may not even be able to touch them without causing some pain, while others may want you yanking on them like a subway strap. Most fellas fall somewhere in the middle of those

"I ONCE SUCKED ON ONE THIS BIG..."

Average length, flaccid dick: 3.5 inches
Average length, erect: 5.1–5.8 inches
Average girth at base of shaft when flaccid: 3.9 inches
Average girth, erect: 4.9 inches
Smokers have smaller erections due to blood constriction.
Smallest functional human penis recorded: 5/8 inch
Largest functional human penis recorded: 11 inches
An 11-inch stack of pennies is equal to: $1.87
Amount of blood in flaccid penis: 1/3 ounce
Amount of blood in erect penis: 3 ounces
Average number of erections per day for a man: 11
Average number of erections while sleeping: 9

Largest penis in the animal kingdom: Blue whale
Length of blue whale penis: 11 feet
An 11-foot stack of pennies equal to: $22.44
Odors that increase blood flow to the penis: lavender, licorice, chocolate, doughnuts, pumpkin pie
Percentage of uncircumcised American males: Approximately 40%
Foreskin Factoid #1: Of the rest, over 99% are circumcised as infants—mostly without anesthesia, thank you.
Foreskin Factoid #2: In the last couple of decades, thousands of foreskins have been sold to biotech labs that need young cells to grow artificial skin for burn victims. One foreskin can be used to grow 250,000 square feet of skin.

extremes, so you'll want to explore them—carefully. But before you do, you need a little biology lesson.

WHERE THE COME COMES FROM

Sperm production takes place in the testicles. Duh. They send the baby spermies to the epididymis, where they mature and are then dumped into the vas deferens. It's the vas deferens that is cut in a vasectomy, keeping the sperm from leaving the testicles. But with no vasectomy, our little spermies are carried to the seminal vesicles and prostate. It's these two guys that manufacture most of the fluid in an ejaculation. The seminal vesicles make two things: (1) A sugar called fructose to nourish the little guys on their way and (2) an enzyme that makes the sperm clump for a while immediately after ejaculating. See, that's because the stupid sperm think they're headed for a vagina and, once deposited there, don't want to be sucked out by the thrusting action of the penis, so they clump. A few minutes later, a time-delay enzyme the prostate adds to the mix liquefies the globs so the sperm can start swimming like mad for the egg. (Shh, if you won't tell them, we won't.) That liquefying enzyme is why you wake up in a puddle half an hour after he came on you. Bet you had no idea it was this complicated, huh? Fortunately, the main thing we're interested in here is making all this happen with our mouths. So let's get back to the cock.

SIZING IT UP

The taboo surrounding dick size has more baggage than Grand Central Station. We've all heard the "big hands + big feet = big dick" theory. Some people swear by it, but it has been scientifically disproved, so you can stop asking the guy you're hitting on for his shoe size. How big he is in the non-aroused state isn't going to tip you off, either, no matter how hard you look at his basket. There are show-ers and there are grow-ers. The size of a man's flaccid penis is no indication of how big it will be when it gets hard. (Of course, if it is impressive limp, it's sure as hell not going to get *smaller.*) Now that we know that, perhaps we can stop looking at men's crotches. Right! Like that would stop us!

Every guy wants to believe his wally is massive and powerful, so you'll need to be respectful of this sad little fact. Many men believe having a massive dick means they are massively masculine or desirable or don't have to reciprocate or take out the trash or some other such bullshit. The reality is that having a massive dick means only one thing: He's a freak. Not that we're against colossal cocks—no, no, no! But statistically speaking, they're just not normal. A whopping 85% of men have between four to seven inches in length. If anything, a really honking big wiener can be a literal pain in the neck because it may not all fit in your mouth, no matter how hard you work at taking it. That means he may not get that lovely sensation of having his whole cock in your mouth. It's a situation that definitely gives a Middle Man, and his smaller (but equally masculine) friends, an advantage.

Now, the average penis is slightly over five inches long, measured along the top from the base (where it starts at the abdomen) to the tip. The average diameter is about 1.5 inches, which makes for a circumference (girth) of around five inches. That said, there is great and glorious variation in size, shape, curvature, shape, length-to-girth and shaft-to-head ratios, hairiness, kind of skin, amount of skin (including foreskin), color(s) and, last but not least, yummy areas of wildly differing sensitivity you're going to learn all about here in this book and "on the job."

Guys are always wanting to know what they can do to make their dick look bigger without surgery, and there are really only two things. One, lose weight. The pubic area (or mons) is all fatty tissue. If a guy is overweight, the mons expands just like his belly, and it hides some of the base of the penis. So if he's going in for lipo anyway, tell him to have that area sucked flat. The other thing he can do is shave. Getting the pubic hair out of the way enables *all* of however much he's got to show *to* show. It can also add some increased sensitivity to his pubic area. But if either of you are uncomfortable with the prepubescent look, try a nice trim instead.

HEAVY METAL

These days you may encounter piercings, so be prepared. The most popular is a Prince Albert, or PA, which is a ring or bent barbell that goes in the urethra and comes out through a piercing in the frenulum. There can be rings through the underside of the shaft as well as through the head. If it pierces the head from side to side, it's an ampalling. If it pierces it from top to bottom, it's an apadravya. Feel free to bring these terms up in conversation and watch most people squirm. In terms of your hummer, there are several considerations. First of all, has the piercing healed? It can take up to a year for an ampalling or apadravya, and several weeks for a PA to heal. The main risk with a still-healing piercing is hepatitis and maybe HIV. Even fully healed, you may find them getting in the way if they are large, and there's nothing like a chipped tooth to take the spark out of the evening. You may need to ask him if he can remove the piercing for the night. If he can't, you can either consider it a challenge or move on to another activity. Can you say hand job? Bringing a hefty dick to climax in your hand is nothing to sneeze at, either—and trust us, as long as he gets off, he won't complain.

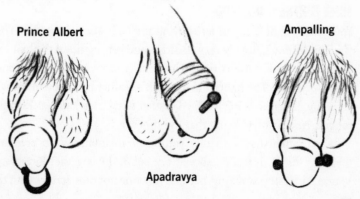

Prince Albert

Ampalling

Apadravya

DRIVING AN ECONOMY MODEL

A quick note about dicks that are not so hefty. Let's just call 'em what they are: small. If you come across one, consider yourself lucky, because it'll make the blow job a lot easier than grappling with some monster. Always remember too that it's attached to a real live person, someone you found sweet and/or hot enough to get down on your knees for in the first place. Besides, why should you buy into our society's bullshit that bigger always means better? We don't know about you, but we've had just as much fun in a VW Beetle as we've had in a Lincoln Town Car.

While we're on the subject of size, we need to include Tim and Tommy Testicles in this discussion. Ball size varies greatly too, and it has nothing to do with the size of the person. Big guys can be pea-size, and a little guy may clang when he walks. The size doesn't correspond to virility or sperm count. Your man can have bull's balls and still be infertile, while the man with the teeny testes could repopulate the state with one load. And with some states, that's not such a bad idea. The testicles also produce testosterone, which brings out a male's secondary sexual characteristics. You know, like facial hair, body hair, temporal baldness, a deep voice, sex drive, and a desire to smash empty beer cans against his forehead. A guy only has to have one testicle to do all that too. Cool, huh?

SOME FURTHER, UH, TIPS

You might want to consider shaving the balls also. *Carefully,* thank you! His nuts are already very sensitive, and getting rid of the hair can heighten sensation dramatically. Suddenly, every square centimeter of skin is exposed. The lightest touch with a feather becomes amazingly arousing. Imagine being touched by that terrific testicular tickler, the tongue. And just try saying that five times fast.

If your man had difficulty getting or maintaining an erection, there are three things he should try before hitting the doc up for Viagra. First, stop smoking, because nicotine not only screws with the nervous system, it clogs the blood vessels he needs to get hard. Men who smoke are nearly twice as likely to have erectile issues as those who don't. That's not just us saying that, that's the Centers for Disease Control and Prevention in Atlanta, pumpkin. Secondly, he could cut out the Häagen-Dazs. Fatty foods also clog arteries, *all* arteries, so if the blood can't get through those arteries in his dick, he's gonna stay soft. So eat low-fat, already. And thirdly, he needs to move his ass to some Janet. Or Beastie Boys or Limp Bizkit—whatever gets his body movin' and groovin'. (OK, maybe *not* Limp Bizkit.) Or play tennis or bike or do some other aerobic-type exercise. As they say, "What's good for your heart is good for your part."

That's a pretty good overview that should get you started exploring the landscape of your man's crotch. Betcha didn't think there was that much to play with down there, huh? If we've done this right, you should feel knowledgeable about the basic area, have a decent understanding of how the machinery works, and not be intimidated by it all. What we want is to sweep away all the negative feelings, everything from "Eww!" and "What the hell is *that*?" to "Oh, God, am I doing it right?" When you're done with this, you *will* be doing it right for three reasons: (1) Because expert cocksuckers are going to share everything they know with you; (2) because we're gonna take it step-by-step; and (3) because we give homework, and you're gonna practice till you drive him crazy. So don't worry about it.

The basic trick is to get into whatever he's got, or ain't got. That is step 1 to the perfect blow job. If he's got hair halfway up his shaft, you need to find that viral and sexy. If he's shaved his privates smoother than a 10-year-old, learn to see it as kinky and fun. If he bends like a boomerang, enjoy the sensations in your throat as you seek to find the most accommodating position. If there are two inches of foreskin overhang, dig in and chow down on it all the more. Hell, if the guy has three balls, imagine how much testosterone must be surging through a manly man like that! What we're trying to say is that, from the giver's point of view, it's all mental anyway. Get to a place where you are comfortable with sucking this particular guy's knob, because you do have a choice. You can decide to approach this with a positive sense of sexy fun and adventure that will give you both a great time, or you can wrinkle your nose because he has too much of this or not enough of that and make you each wish you were watching C-SPAN. It's up to you. What kind of attitude are you going to bring to the party?

QUICKIE QUIZ
Should You Be Allowed to Read the Rest of This Book?

1. What is it that makes a man's penis jerk upward?
A. The suspensory ligaments.
B. That tickling thing you do with your tongue.
C. Ramming an ampalling through it.

2. That little area under the head where the foreskin is/was attached is called:
A. The frenulum or frenum.
B. Who cares, as long as I remember to play with it when I'm down there!
C. Wanda.

3. The tunica albuginea is:
A. What fills with blood, making the dick hard.
B. Today's menu special, served with risotto and garlic bread.
C. Not a term I'm ever likely to have to say, so leave me the fuck alone.

4. The average penis is:
A. A little over five inches long and about five inches around when erect.

B. Way fun. Why else are we here?

C. Over nine inches long and barely able to fit in your mouth! (Well, that's what you say about his average penis, anyway.)

5. A corona is:

A. The ridge around the base of the glans.

B. What I'm gonna lick.

C. An imported beer that's good with a squeeze of lime.

6. The penis gets hard because it is filled with the man's:

A. Blood.

B. Testosterone.

C. Ego.

7. After coming, a man needs time to get hard again. That's called:

A. The refractory period.

B. The OK-you-had-yours-now-you-do-me time.

C. *The Simpsons*.

8. An uncircumcised man has:

A. Foreskin.

B. Dick cheese.

C. Little chance of speaking Hebrew.

9. A small, flaccid penis means:

A. Nothing, other than this penis is small when not hard.

B. You're not doing your job.

C. The water is very, very cold.

10. Care must be taken with the testicles because:

A. They are very tender.

B. They are still illegal in some states.

C. They can fall off and roll under the sofa.

SCORING

OK, the correct answers were all "A." If you had any "B" answers, you may want to go back and reread this chapter. (It's all about dick, so why should you mind?) If you had any "C" answers, you're a complete moron and should immediately put this book back on the shelf and never, ever even try to give head. For the rest of you, find yourself a willing male of the human species and spend some time with his privates. (We told you we gave homework.) Get to know what's sensitive and where that is on your man. This is just for you to familiarize yourself with all the areas you've been learning about and help you to identify places that perhaps you didn't even know had names. And don't worry about performance anxiety. We're not asking you to open wide just yet, although if you feel so inspired, go ahead. Who are we to stop a little extracurricular activity?

3

HOT SPOTS

Still with us? Good. We were afraid some of you would jump the gun and dive for your partner's crotch after that last chapter. All that talk about dick definitely got *us* a tad distracted. However, there are still a few more things you need to know before you can successfully smoke his sex cigar like a pro.

Getting comfortable with his cock and balls was just the beginning. We know it's hard to believe, but guys also like to have other parts of their bodies fondled. Your job—but a fun job at that—is to find these hot spots. While your last boyfriend may have enjoyed you sucking his nipples so hard you could have extracted milk, your current snookums may feel little sensation in that area—or find it painful or extremely ticklish. Same things goes for the areas you'll be exploring while you're nestled between his thighs.

And while we'd love to encourage y'all to think of the entire body as one big erogenous zone, let's be realistic, shall we? If you're focusing on licking his lollipop (which is kinda what we are here to talk about) it's difficult to push every button he has available to push. To go from giving head to kissing to nibbling his ear to intercourse takes away from your mission: to make the blow job the main event.

There are a significant number of men out there who can't come from somebody bobbing on their boner. Well, at least they *think* they can't. That's the reason hummers get demoted to something you do before you slap on a rubber and screw. Most likely it's

30%

of men feel that they come too soon.

because focusing on cleaning his love gun isn't enough. If that's the case, you're just gonna have to take matters into your own hands. Literally.

Your hands are useful for a lot of things. Writing, climbing up ladders, opening doors, pinching your boyfriend's ass, picking your nose, and yes, even turning the pages of this smart-ass book. They're also pretty handy at helping bring your macho man (or men!) to climax. The one-two punch of having his dick in your mouth along with getting his inner thighs stroked may do it. Or maybe you'll have to finger his asshole to get him gushing. Whatever it takes, there are enough extra goodies within arm's reach to play with to have your blow job become a cocksucking career.

IT'S THIGH TIME

As the blood starts flowing to his man missile, the entire surrounding region becomes highly sensitive—especially his thighs. Most of you have probably had the pleasure of wearing shorts or boxers and having someone start rubbing or feeling around your upper leg. It's an added sensation to have someone rub their finger along and slightly inside the edge of your briefs, if that's what you're sporting. This kind of teasing is great for pre-oral foreplay. Everything from a gentle caress to a deep massage can feel good round these parts; it all depends on what he's in the mood for. Here are a few things you'll want to try next time you're polishing his trophy:

1. Keep his boxers on and pull his little friend (although we'd suggest calling it his big friend—remember the ego) out of the slot in front. While your mouth and one of your hands are busy working his woody, slip the other hand up under the underwear. The rubbing will feel great, but this move will also cause some tension in the boxers, affecting the entire groin area. In essence, it's like you're giving his whole midsection a mild squeeze. This works even better if you learn

to suck well enough to get both hands freed and roaming around his upper legs.

2. Don't forget that the back of his thighs are sensitive as well. Rubbing the area just under his butt cheeks will get the blood flowing there—which will prepare him if you decide to slip your finger or a sex toy up his ass a little later.

3. If (or more like *when*) you want to take a breather, continue the motion by giving him a temporary hand job and lick around the scrotum. Again, this technique is all about "teasing" him, because you're just dancing around his bat and balls. The sensations a wet tongue evokes feel good (oh, really?) but are usually not intense enough to bring him to orgasm. However, this'll prolong the blow job, stimulate even more nerves, *and* give you time to rest. Talk about multitasking!

BUTT, BUTT, BUTT...

While those of us who have experienced the pleasures of butt love were content to let you naysayers wander about in ignorance, we decided that since we were talking about forging new sexual frontiers *anyway,* we'd give you all one more chance to explore the back door.

Obviously, you're aware that the anus is located mere inches behind his (or your) dick. It's no mistake that these two are neighbors. While they're both there to get rid of unwanted waste from your body, when used in conjunction they have the potential to give a guy some of the most intense orgasms he'll ever experience.

First off, though, we'd like to trash any myths, preconceptions, or just plain idiotic notions a lot of you still carry around regarding anal penetration for men. This is mostly for the hetero audience out there, but we know some of you fags have some hang-ups as well about *anal*-ysis, so it wouldn't hurt (oops, sorry) to find out the facts.

For you breeder boys out there, no, getting pleasure from having a finger or dildo or butt plug or any other object stuck up your ass does not mean you're gay. As for you homos, nor does it imply that you are less of a man or whatever other bullshit you'd like to believe. What it does mean is that you have a rear that is loaded with nerves that are responsive to all sorts of prodding. It could also mean that your prostate gland is healthy and functioning. Basically, your cute buns are just a pleasure center waiting to be tapped.

That's where your partner comes in, figuratively speaking. We tried to deal with most of the "issues" back in chapter 1, so we promise not to dwell on this too long. We're cognizant of the fact that most ladies don't really think too much about sticking things up their boyfriend's butts. That's cool. Yet there's a lot of literature (and we mean *truckloads*) on how great anal penetration is for men. To put it bluntly, it's not just for "exiting," as a lot of guys are prone to say. And while, biologically speaking, his body is rarin' to have you do some tunneling, psychologically he may not be prepared. That's why *you* have to be.

Trust us, if you go slowly, after a few times and a bottle of lube, he can be taking your finger with no problems. Hell, you might get two or three up there—but right now we're just trying to get one in the door. Your man is putting a lot of trust in you by getting him to this point. Think back to your first time. (Unless your "real" first time sucked, then think back to your first *good* lay.) Remember how he really was into it, and even if you were hesitant, the thought of pleasing him made you happy? Go into this with the same mentality. We're not telling you to strap on a dildo and pillage his ass (well, not yet). Instead, let him know that you've done your research. If he's one of those that freaks out about it being a "gay thing," tell him you read about it in *Cosmo* or *Men's Health*. If he trusts you (which he does) and you're enthusiastic about doing it (which you are), it should be a walk in the park. The biggest barrier isn't his sphincter muscle, it's in his head. Once you get him comfortable, both mentally and physically, we guarantee there's a good chance this will make him want more.

Same thing goes for you queers who think your asshole is off limits. While coming from a basic blow job is definitely possible, why do you think your partner enjoys getting plowed by you? Uh, we thinks because it feels good. We'd hate to destroy all the misconceptions you "tops" have, so we'll just put being on the receiving end out as a suggestion. You can either heed our advice or die never knowing the joys of having that hot beefcake in your bed stick his thumb up your Stair-Mastered ass as he sucks your stiff rod until you shoot over your head. Sigh. It sure sounds depressing to us.

Anyway, let's get back to roasting his weenie and how his manly backside fits into the equation. We've already mentioned the lube, trust, the lube, timing, relaxation, and the lube. Did you get the part about the lube? And, again, make sure it's water-based and free of irritants like nonoxynol-9.

Now you find yourself slurping away at his grade AA beef, and after some massaging you run your finger down to his anus and put some pressure on it. He'll tell you to stop, but just slap him and shove your finger right on up there. Just kidding. If he knows that you're going to try it (communication!), it's your duty to make sure he's relaxed and that your finger is lubricated. (Oh, and you'll want to file down the nails, if you have any. Ouch!)

49% of men prefer to perform oral sex on a circumcised penis.

Most of you probably know that the sphincter is a muscle, and it works just like any other muscle in the human body. The pressure you're applying to his asshole feels good because of the nerves. Attempting to get *inside* may hurt because he's too tense or you're moving too quickly. Giving him head will help with the relaxation, but it's up to you to be patient and slowly work your finger up inside him. Read his body language. Ask him if it hurts. It'll probably be uncomfortable the first few times, but so is running and lifting weights. It just takes a little bit of practice to get used to it.

Aside from fingers, a host of other fun things can be used to stimulate your man while you're going down on him. For the more advanced, there are butt plugs, anal beads, and dildos, all of which come in different sizes (and colors, if you're obsessive like that) for whatever level on which you are playing. We'll discuss these in further detail a little later.

What's more, while he's into getting his ass explored, you may want to try some rimming. If you need a short break, keep jacking him off (or have him do it himself) and push his legs up toward his head. While rimming someone doesn't appeal to everyone, we have yet to hear of a man, gay or straight, who doesn't enjoy having his ass eaten out. Again, it's mostly about the pressure and slick feeling of a warm tongue that make this so pleasurable. If you find that he digs it more than you thought, incorporate it into your sexual repertoire. Right now we're going to get back to BJs.

When you finally do work anal probing into your suck-off sessions, remember that it'll probably be a rather intense orgasm for him. (You didn't think millions of gay men enjoyed getting fucked just to piss off the religious right, did ya?) After he comes, be aware that it'll be slightly painful to withdraw your finger or whatever from his ass. You may even want to take it out right before he's about to shoot or while he's in the process. Whatever he prefers, natch.

TUMMY RUB

They say one of the ways to a man's heart is through his stomach. Well, during a romp you pretty much figure that his heart (and brain) have probably migrated to his pecker—and we're sure that they took his stomach right along with them. (Why do you think they call it a sexual appetite?)

Once you've got him worked up, rub your hand over his stomach in a random fashion. Keep him guessing where the next touch is going to come from. In fact, start to alternate between these three new stimulus regions. Rub his thighs, then his stomach, followed by a gentle poke or lick at his asshole. Again, you can take a few minutes to let your jaw muscles recover or to accumulate some more spit. Kiss his stomach or, while jacking him off, go up and give him a passionate kiss on the lips. All this attention and moving around let him know that you are really into what you're doing.

THE NIPPLE EFFECT

And if you can reach, a lot of guys enjoy some nipple play. However, it's a stretch for a lot of people while they're down between his legs, so it'd be wise to let him tweak and pinch his own nipples. It shouldn't really matter as long as they're getting stimulated and he continues to emit lots of growls and moans.

But if you can reach, or figure some way to incorporate them into the oral sex play, the nipples are a nice example of how more subtle erogenous zones can add to the overall intensity. Aside from the standard pinching and pulling (which can feel anything but "standard") with your fingers, it might be cool to stuff his stocking with some nipple clamps this Christmas. Hey, it sure beats coal (and socks).

Nipple clamps are really just modified clothespins. You'll probably want to start off with tweezer clamps, which allow you to adjust the strength of the pinch. Over time, though, you can go from loose to the point where the clamps make your nipples perkier than Britney Spears's.

And just how does this make licking his stick all the more magnificent? Actually, it helps in a couple of ways. Firstly, the clamps can take care of his chest region nerves, which leaves your hands open to exploring other areas that need to be rubbed. However, most of these devices have a chain linking the two clamps, so all you have to do is tug on the chain (but not too hard). Secondly, it's a good way to test his pain threshold, just in case you'd like to throw some S/M or other "it hurts so good" techniques into the mix. Finally,

100

approx. cost in dollars spent on a year's worth of condoms by a sexually active man.

17%

of straight men have had 20 or more sexual partners since age 18.

nipple clamps are just one of the tools used in the domination scene; it gives more "power" to the giver, which he may find a hot change of pace if he's a control freak.

Some things you should know: (1) Like some beauty products, it's not smart to leave clamps on for more than 15 minutes at a time. (2) If the pain is more of a "hurting" pain than a "pleasurable" pain, it doesn't take a genius to figure out that you should stop. Otherwise, enjoy the clampdown.

HAIR APPARENT

If you're one of those fellas that shaves your body (or you're dating one), it's too bad. Hair tugging is another way to inflict pleasant pain on your man. We've already gone over all the areas you can play with, but the hair on the inner thigh can easily be lightly yanked to fire off some of the nerves down there. Also, don't forget his treasure trail or maybe even his butt hair, if he has any.

LUBE JOB

OK, so sue us, but as gay men we firmly believe that you can never have (or use) enough lube. While it's obviously necessary for any anal penetration, some lubricants are made especially for use on the skin. Hot/cold lube is cool because when you rub it in it'll heat up the area—and then you can blow on it for an almost instant opposite extreme.

Certain scented oils not only make the massaging go more smoothly, but as we pointed out in the previous chapter, certain aromas (like lavender) can actually get a guy even more turned on (as if you swinging from his pole wasn't enough).

A word of warning, though: Make sure that the products you're using won't harm you if you ingest them. There's a very good chance that you'll probably lick some of it off him, and it would, uh, blow if right before you're about to make him fire his rounds you need to be rushed to the hospital. Nothing kills the moment faster than having to be rushed away in an ambulance.

"I DON'T WANT TO GROW UP..."

Although playing with your old GI Joes (or Barbies, as the case may be) is considered pretty weird now that you're in your 30s, you can still be a Toys "R" Us kid in the bedroom. A few pages back we hastily listed a bunch of items like butt plugs and dildos as if they were common, everyday words. (Well, they are for us.) Anyway, that was just to throw some of you more conservative types off, although if you want to know the truth, it's usually you uptight Republican wankers that are the most perverted behind closed doors. We guess having ice water for blood does that to ya.

It's up to you and your partner to decide which ones work best, both in giving the receiver pleasure and as easy-to-manipulate tools that the giver can use without straining themselves. A beginner will probably want to start off with a small butt plug of some sort. It'll help you learn to relax your sphincter without the possible added stress of having something constantly moved in and out of your ass.

Dildos are also nifty to play with during oral sex. Like butt plugs, they vary in size and shape (sort of like actual dicks) but can also provide that extra charge if they take batteries. We're only going to mention these two, because something like anal beads requires concentration and patience. However, if you do become (or already are) some sort of super sex ninja, who are we to stop you from shoving whatever size sex toys he can take up your boyfriend's backside?

Well, there you have it. With all the things you can yank, it's no wonder he'll soon be your little lust puppet. The key to keeping him a *wood*-en boy is not to try everything out all at once. Well, unless you're only keeping him around for one night. But if you're looking for that second date it's always a good rule of thumb to have a few tricks that you can pull from the ol' hat. What's more, if he proves to be relationship material, well, you're gonna need a helluva lot more than a few moves. That's why we suggest trying out variations on all of these hot spots as well as the techniques and positions we'll be offering up in a few pages.

4

HEAD OF THE CLASS

Now that you have a pretty solid understanding of the major players in his pecker—not to mention all the nifty areas within arm's reach that you can massage, pull, and poke—it's time for a little pep talk. In the ensuing chapters you're gonna pick up some useful techniques and positions to try out on your boy toy. But first, we're going to make sure that you're in the right mind-set. And what better way to do that than with true tales of how these five men and women became blow job kings and queens!

Even if you're rarin' to rip off his undies right now, being horny is only part of the equation for giving a quality pole polishing. Having your motor revving helps, sure, but it really only gives you motivation. What if you're sucking off somebody who's never ejaculated from a blow job? And we're sure some of you have been attracted to someone only to find out that they won't reciprocate or, worse, that they just lie there without giving much response or guidance.

If you're serious about becoming a blow job Jedi Master, then as with anything physical, you need to make sure your *mental* state is in good standing. Remember, this isn't only about stealing your partner in cocksucking crime's load, it's about *you* getting off too. Shocking, we know, but oral sex is supposed to be fun for both (or should we say all?) parties involved. So, before we delve into the when, where, and what of oral sex, here are some inspiring accounts of *how* a handful of dubious dick suckers became members of the royal court.

WHAT IS LOVE?

"I used to dread giving my boyfriends head," says 35-year-old Monique, a successful lawyer and single mother of one. "I went through this streak in my 20s where I felt that I needed to be in a relationship. I didn't want to be single, so if I broke up with one man, I'd be dating a new one within a week. It wasn't so much for the sex as it was for the security. What's more, I think these guys sensed my desperation and took advantage of my need to be in a relationship. Don't get me wrong, I wasn't throwing myself at their feet looking for approval. If he ended up being a total jerk, I'd kick him to the curb. But most of them were decent—except when it came to oral sex.

"It's true, you know, that men want to be sucked off, and they'll do whatever needs to be done to get some. I always saw going down as a small price to pay to have somebody to sleep next to and go to movies with. You lick his dick for a few minutes, you fuck, he comes, and he's content for a day or two. Simple enough, right?

"Wrong. I'd been out of law school for about five years when I met Matt. He was handsome, successful, and for once in my dating life, wasn't trying to play any games with me. I picked him up about four days after breaking up with some guy whose name I forget. I was out with two of my girlfriends and after chatting for a while he offered to drive me home, which was cool because I was pretty drunk.

"You know what happens next? He drops me off at my house and gives me a kiss good night. He was hot and I was slightly horny, so I asked him if he wanted to have a nightcap. He smiled and declined,

23,000
approx. number of penile implants in use in the U.S.

saying he'd give me a call the next day so we could go on a 'proper' date. I'll have to admit, I was a bit let down and didn't really get a good night's sleep. But the next day he called me, and after four dates (a personal best for me) we finally jumped in the sack. Before I could go down on him, though, he decided to take control and started exploring *my* body. He tongued and sucked my breasts for a while, then fingered me while he licked up and down my thighs. Eventually he started eating me out, but the thing I remember most is that he kept coming back to kiss me on the lips.

"He was really into pleasing me, so when I finally pushed him on his back and took his dick in my hand I realized that I'd never seen a man's penis as being something sexy. But as I looked up at Matt, as I started to lick the head of his cock, he smiled down at me like he was saying 'Thank you.' Not only did his erect dick turn me on, but so did his chest and stomach hair, which I never cared much about before. Instead of rushing to get it over with, I found myself enjoying the taste of his dick in my mouth and the feel of his balls in my hands as I tugged and rubbed them. I even got hot and bothered by the smell of his crotch.

"I seriously gave him an hour-long blow job that night. He kept telling me how great it felt and touching me gently with his big hands. It was the first time I ever made a guy come just through oral sex, but it definitely wasn't my last time with Matt. He and I ended up staying together for three years, and I always enjoyed giving him head."

IN MONIQUE'S OWN WORDS: "With Matt I figured out that, for me, enjoying oral sex was about loving someone. I'd been with so many guys that I just *liked* that sex, especially hummers, were just obligatory foreplay. I've been single for the past four months and it's fine. I've been out on a few dates, but I have my friends and, above all, my son, Kyle, to keep me company. I'm sure another 'Matt' will come my way, and when he does I'm looking forward to enjoying again just how sexy a guy's body, and dick, can be."

THE BOTTOM LINE: Even oral sex is a two-way street. The person doing the sucking has got to be into it just as much as the guy that dick is attached to. Think about this: Say your lover wants to go to a concert, but you can't stand the band he wants to see. You'll go, sure, to show you support him. But what if he wanted to do this two times a week? It'd start to wear on your nerves pretty quickly, huh? We say screw the notion that it's all about pleasing him. Find a way to make it enjoyable for you too. For Monique, as we're sure it is for a lot of you out there, that means caring for the person. And no matter what your bitter, jaded friends tell you, enjoying oral sex with someone you love is totally acceptable. Besides, they're just jealous that you're gettin' some.

ALL GROWN UP

"When sex became more than just about getting off," admits Jarod, a 24-year-old graduate student, "that's when I discovered that giving head was more than a segue into butt love.

"After I finished my undergrad work I took a year off to work and decide if I really wanted to go to grad school. I'd been sexually active since high school, but it was in college that I really went wild. Not totally crazy, but I was so excited to be away from home and on my own. I felt so adult, and luckily, I was secure in my sexuality. I liked guys, and to suddenly be surrounded by thousands of hotties my age got me going. Plus, I spent all four of my college years in a fraternity. I never got with any of my brothers, but I did screw around with quite a few guys from other frats.

" 'Screw around' is the perfect phrase too. I wasn't looking to get into a relationship or anything, and neither were any of the guys I fucked on a regular basis. Blow jobs were always popular. You could keep most of your clothes on, and they didn't require the privacy and physical investment that sex did. See, I didn't even consider giving or getting head as sex. We were horny college kids, but sex was for relationships. None of the frat boys would even dare to be in a relationship. Blow jobs were between 'buddies.'

"After I graduated I moved into a one-bedroom apartment and got a job. It was then that I actually started dating other out guys and I started investing more in sex. I had an apartment to myself, so I didn't have to worry about somebody barging in on me anymore. Of course, I didn't have access to the frequent blow jobs, so there was definitely a downside to living alone. However, about two months after graduation this guy picks me up at a gay bar in San Francisco. Oh, I forgot to mention that I went to Berkeley, right? Anyway, my apartment is in the City, so we head back to my place. I hadn't gotten laid in over a month, so I was about to explode.

early morning

the most arousing time of day for a man: Hormone levels peak.

"Back at my place we chatted for a few minutes, then this guy—Greg was his name—leaned over and kissed me. In about five minutes all of our clothes were off and we're rolling around on my floor, kissing and rubbing our hands all over each other. After a little of this he stood up and took me over to the couch. He sat me down and started sucking on my dick. It was amazing. He would speed up and slow down, then firmly grasp my dick while he licked the head. You could tell he'd been doing this for years.

"He was so good, in fact, that after five minutes I was ready to shoot. He noticed that I was getting close, so he stopped and stood up. He had a huge dick, probably about nine inches, and as I moved forward to start sucking him off he forcefully grabbed the back of my head. I started beating myself off, but Greg noticed this and whispered 'No you don't' and grabbed my arm. He put both of my hands on his dick and started pumping gently into them.

"I'd dealt with big dicks before, but all of those guys would just lay back, not feeling that they had to participate or whatever. But Greg took the initiative. He didn't want to just get off, he wanted me to enjoy his entire cock. In the beginning I sucked and stroked frantically, eager to make him come. He wouldn't have any of this, though, and kept making me slow down.

"After about half an hour my jaw started to get sore, so we went to my bedroom and Greg laid me down on my bed and started sucking on my balls. All the while he had one hand slowly stroking my dick while a finger from the other was pressing gently on my asshole. He had all three going at once, and it was so intense, I don't think I could have mustered up the concentration necessary to shoot my load. The tag-team sucking went on for almost four hours, and when I finally did come, I felt some of it hit my face—the only other time I'd done that was when I was getting fucked."

IN JAROD'S OWN WORDS: "Basically, I grew up. After Greg I realized that sex, especially oral sex, didn't have to be about finishing up in five minutes or less. I loved sucking dick when I was in college, but it was more about quantity than quality back then. When I realized that I wasn't trying to set some land-speed record while sucking on some guy's tool, I found out how hot blow jobs can really be."

THE BOTTOM LINE: Take your time. Quickies are fine once in a while, but if you don't rush, you can explore his body and pick up on some of his responses. Even if it's just a one-night stand, is it really worth it to get all spruced up, buy him drinks, and chat with him all night just for five minutes of fellatio?

NO END IN SIGHT

"I don't want to come off as sounding shallow," declares Dennis, a 32-year-old architect from the Bay Area, "but sex is mostly about the end result for me. I can have sex for hours or minutes, but I love to see men come. It's intimate, it's messy, and it shows how all the hard work has paid off. However, rarely am I able to come from being blown. Well, until I met Carl.

"Back in 1998 I think I had pretty much slept with about every gay guy in San Francisco. Well, at least every *other* gay guy. Anyway, I had also enjoyed just about every kind of sex, from vanilla to group to sex in a sling. I've always been sexually adventurous, but after sucking off this guy I'd met at a party one night and watching him come after only a few minutes, I realized two things: (1) He wasn't getting a second date, and (2) I'd never come from being blown. I was shocked at first, seeing as I'd done just about everything you could possibly do in the buff—with the exception of some of the more extreme things, like fisting. It seemed so basic to have ejaculated while someone was pumping your rod, but when I thought back, I remembered either coming while fucking or while jacking myself off.

"Carl was the ex of an acquaintance of mine, and we knew each other from the neighborhood bars and a few get-togethers we'd both attended. He was about 10 years older than me, so I never thought there was any physical attraction. He was all muscly and dark-featured, while I was toned and blond. To make a long story short, we ended up going back to his place one night after a dinner at his ex's. We'd both walked there and had been talking about music and he said he wanted to show me some of his 'old records.' Uh-huh, we all know what that means. Of course, we end up having sex, and while we're sixty-nining each other I start thinking about wanting to come just from getting head. Carl turned out to be a lot hotter naked than I thought he'd be, and he was obviously into me.

17

average age a man has his first sexual experience

"Eventually he started to finger me while he sucked, and I started to do the same to him. Well, I could feel myself getting close, which was usually the time I started taking matters into my own hands, if you know what I mean. Carl sensed it and started sucking harder and stuck two fingers up my ass. By now we weren't in the sixty-nine position anymore—he was standing on the ground while my legs dangled off his bed (which was pretty high off the ground). His motions were smooth and tight, but I just couldn't come. I moved my hand down to start stroking myself, but he pushed my hand away and continued on doing what he was doing.

"Obviously, I started to get a little nervous. I knew Carl wanted to make me orgasm, but I was thinking too much about it to let him finish me off. My body language changed or something, because Carl suddenly stopped and grabbed my hand so I could start beating off. However, he put his hand over mine and made me go slow while he went up and down with his mouth, mimicking the motion of our hands. As I got closer to shooting my load I started to speed up, and Carl kept up with my pace; it was like we were both sharing control.

"I began to tense up, but before the point of no return, Carl subtly removed my hand and continued on with his blow job. Rather than finger my ass or play with my balls at this point, all his focus went to my dick, like it would be if I were jacking off. I put my right hand on his head so I could still feel that movement, and two minutes later I was coming in Carl's mouth. It was like discovering the joys of sex all over again."

IN DENNIS'S OWN WORDS: "Carl and I continued to hook up about once a week for five months after that night. Basically, he slowly weaned me off of my habit of making myself come rather than letting the other person accomplish the mission. On that first night he read my body language and knew what he needed to do to make me come. Nowadays, thanks to that stud, just about anybody who can give decent head can make me shoot, although I'm trying to figure out if there are any other basic sexual pleasures I have yet to experience."

THE BOTTOM LINE: Simple: Find a partner who is responsive to your needs. But just as Carl included Dennis (or at least his hand) in the sex play, Dennis was aware that his partner wanted to make him orgasm. Carl also enjoyed the end result, so they compromised without even talking—and Dennis had another "first time."

ALL TIED UP

All the stories up to this point have been about looking at blow jobs in a different light. They emphasized discovering something new that the person enjoyed about oral sex. Well, Heather, a 27-year-old bisexual writer, wanted to chat about something she didn't like and how she went about changing it.

"I hate not being in control," she admits. "I also don't like it if the other person is overly passive in response to my assertiveness. Especially during sex, I'm totally turned on by power struggles. But most of the men and women I've slept with have been either too aggressive or too shy to tell me what they really wanted.

"Last year I was dating this stockbroker who I'd met through a friend of mine. He was totally sexy and had a really nice ass. I mean, even straight guys wanted to grab it. All of his money and success and stuff made him pretty self-assured, but he wasn't a jerk about it. Hey, if you've got it, you've got it. Whenever I gave him head he knew I was enjoying it, but I think this made him nervous. I almost always initiated the sucking sessions, which, he told me later, he thought was weird for a girl to do. And while I did like that he talked dirty at times and was a bit forceful, a lot of the times he was *too* forceful.

"One night I was sucking him off in the shower—I love having sex in the shower—and when we get out he carries me over to the bed and throws me on, all wet. He thought he was going to take control of the situation, again, but I was coy and convinced him to lay down on his back. I told him to stay put and hopped off the bed. His dick was as hard as a rock as he put his hands behind his head. I went over to his closet and got two of his stockbroker ties.

" 'What are you doing?' he asked.

" 'You'll see,' I replied.

"I climbed back on his bed and he saw the two ties. He said they were expensive, and I responded by telling him I'd buy him new ones. I then quickly grabbed his arm and knotted one end of the tie around his wrist. I'd never tied him up before, and in the dark I made out a slightly worried expression on his face. I told him to relax, and soon both arms were tied to his bedposts. It was time for me to continue that blow job.

"I spread his legs, got between them, and grasped his cock in my right hand. I think I grabbed it too hard because he jerked, but before he could say anything I was licking the head of his dick. I got him going for about 15 minutes, then slid up to give him a kiss. He instinctively tried to put his arms around me but could barely move them off the bed. I smiled, and he knew that *I* was in control now.

"I turned around so that we were in the sixty-nine position. He started to lick my pussy, but it was obviously difficult for him to do very much. I started deep-throating him—I'm great at doing that—and slowly slid one of my fingers down to his asshole and pressed on it. He froze, stopped what he was doing, and told me that he wasn't into getting his ass fingered. I turned and faced him again.

> # 30%
> **of men say they regularly blow their partner until he comes.**

"'Don't worry,' I whispered. 'I know what I'm doing.'

"I went back to the sixty-nine position, licked my finger, and 10 minutes later I was fingering him. It was amazing. He was totally moaning and I could feel the blood pumping inside his cute ass. It was really tight, and I could tell he was enjoying it. He started eating me out like crazy and before I knew it—I'm not even sure *he* was aware of it—I had two fingers inside him and was moving quickly in and out. His legs stiffened and his come shot out and sprayed in my face. There was tons of it.

"After he stopped quivering, I untied him and we went to take another shower. I watched him walk into the bathroom—he was walking kind of funny—and I liked his ass even more."

IN HEATHER'S OWN WORDS: "A lot of things went on that night. I stripped him of the control he usually had by tying him up but still maintained his trust and got him to experience something he had never experienced before. During our 'cleanup' shower he admitted that getting fingered felt better than he could have imagined. I enjoyed it because I took charge and helped our sex life get to the next level. Plus, he realized that not being 'on top,' that vulnerability, had made the blow job more intense."

THE BOTTOM LINE: First, getting tied up is way hot. Especially if it's a sexy stockbroker with manly buns. Second, in order for your partner to try something new, you have to be both persuasive and self-assured. Don't suggest that he'll like it—*tell* him that he will. Of course, to back up that claim, please know what you're doing. If you don't, trust us, it'll leave a bad first impression and he may never want to try it again.

TALK DIRTY TO ME

"I've always been simple when it comes to sex," says 39-year-old Brett. "I come from a small-town religious family, so even though I was gay, I still felt the need to not focus on sex. Since I couldn't convince myself that sex was to have kids, like my brother and sister did, I figured that it was more about stress relief and love than as something you do for fun. Especially oral sex. Sucking on my partner's penis didn't really appeal to me all that much. We've been together for 14 years, and over the years sex has become something we do once a week. Oral sex is even more infrequent.

"But a few years back, when I turned 36, my hormones suddenly kicked in again. Honestly, I hadn't felt this horny since college. I started noticing other guys around town, and Jack, my partner, was taken aback at the fact that I wanted to have sex four or five times a week. I think it might have been that I'd started exercising again at that time. I was eating healthier and sleeping better at night—which, I've read, increases your sex drive.

"One night Jack and I were watching TV and I got up to get a glass of water. When I came back into the living room I noticed that Jack was sitting there in his underwear, these white boxer briefs. He is five years younger than me, but he still looks like he's in his late 20s. Suddenly I was standing there with a huge hard-on, staring at Jack, who was looking kind of sleepy.

"I walked over to where he was sitting and kneeled down in front of him. I didn't waste any time and started to pull off his underwear.

His eyes widened but he didn't say a word. He got stiff rather quickly, and before I could start sucking him off he reached down and pulled my T-shirt over my head. While I blew him, Jack turned the volume on the TV way down, so all I could hear was his low moans and my slurping. He put one of his hands on my head and said in a low voice, 'Yeah, suck it.'

"I was sort of taken aback because Jack rarely ever talked during sex, and when he did, it was only to ask if I was all right. I kinda wanted to stop, but he pulled my head forward and pushed it down on his dick. He started saying some more things, like 'You want it, don't you?' and he told me to go faster and suck harder. Then he pulled his dick out of my mouth, stood up, and told me to lick his balls.

"I remember I started thinking about the few porn movies I'd seen and how they sort of talked like this. Porn doesn't really turn me on, but because Jack was obviously enjoying the dirty talk, I went along with it. In fact, it was sexy because Jack sounded way more convincing than those porn stars.

"I didn't say a word through the whole thing, which I guess lasted about 30 or 45 minutes. I rimmed him for a few minutes, but it was mostly about the blow job that night. Jack had never been all that forceful, and it took me off guard how something simple like dirty talk could make oral sex that much more enjoyable.

IN BRETT'S OWN WORDS: "Like I said, I have never really been into porn, mostly because the guys I've seen in them seem really detached. Even though Jack was saying some rather pornographic things to me, I knew they were coming from inside. He wanted to be naughty that night, and we've been together for so long, he felt comfortable doing that in front of me. Personally, I was surprised we hadn't done it sooner, but it sure has helped our sex life."

THE BOTTOM LINE: Don't be afraid to try something new in front of your partner. Unless it's way out there, introducing a fantasy or novel dimension can only spice things up. And after 14 years, who doesn't need some new ingredients?

So what should you take away from these five tantalizing tales? Well, for one, oral sex is all about pleasure—and not just for the guy getting blown but for the blowee as well. If you're a guy giving another guy head, well, enjoy it as much as you'd like *him* to when you're gettin' serviced. As for you ladies, realize that dicks can be a lot of fun. They're basically like gear shifts, so the smoother you handle them, the more exhilarating the drive.

5
BLOW HIS MIND

You need to go into this knowing you're going to be spending some time. This book is not about the five-minute backseat boy suck-off. Not that we're against that sort of activity—no, no, no! And we thank those of you who were so accommodating at the end of the night with our car parked in your parents' driveway—not to mention at the interstate rest stops. But that's not what this guide is about. So get into the mind-set that giving head is a good, *lo-o-ong* way of pleasuring the man you've selected to be your partner (or for the night). If he's good enough to go down on, he's good enough for you to take the time to show him that you know what you're doing.

You're ready to start sucking cock. Great, but let's consider for a moment just what sucking means. You're creating a vacuum, and there are gradations of that, going from light suction all the way up to the Hoover Black Hole Super Suck. There's sucking on a particular area or part, such as the head of the penis, or the delicate sucking on a testicle, which is something else entirely. There's sucking on the whole dick, or with both balls in your mouth, or on some more specific region, like the perineum. You remember the perineum from chapter 2, right? Obviously, different parts are going to be able to withstand different intensities, depending on sensitivity.

The trick, as always, is to *pay attention to his reaction*. You may be saying, "No shit, Sherlock." But sometimes you can get so into what you think you're doing ("Oh, I am so great at this. He's gotta be impressed!") that you aren't reading his signs. There's the moan of "Don't stop!" and the cry of "Don't! *Stop!*" There's squirming in pleasure, and there's squirming to try and get away from your jaws of death. What feels great on the glans can be catastrophic on the *cojones*. Be attentive. Especially if he's into a little pain, because there's the "hurts so good" kind of pain and then there's just plain ol' pain pain. Nobody wants that. Well, maybe that sideshow freak we saw lifting cinder blocks with his tongue at the circus last week, but he also had 97% of his body covered in prison tattoos.

Usually a quick glance at his face is enough to check in. If you two are doing it in the dark, listen to the noises he makes. And you can always ask, "Is that OK?" Remember, if this is your first blow job with this cutie, you're not only learning his likes but his limits. If you have sodomized him a few times, you may want to push those limits. That's cool, but do it slowly and carefully, all the while keeping tabs on how he reacts. As a rule of thumb, screaming in agony is not a good sign.

SLIP-SLIDING AWAY

Since his penis is going to be sliding in and out of your mouth, you need to get used to this concept. That motion is going to be happening a lot with each mouth-fuck session. It's also going to be pretty rough unless you can muster up some spit. Saliva is your friend. Don't be afraid of it. Use a lot, because it tends to dry out pretty quickly, and we don't want that, do we? Don't worry about slobbering, either. Emily Post does not apply when you're sucking cock.

Spit is your natural lubricant, so use it to make sliding that man meat in and out a lot easier. Get that dick slick. It's good for (literally) blowing on too, to give his dick a cool chill before you take him back in your oh-so-warm-and-moist mouth. That little trick can also delay orgasm if you want to make him wait longer. More on that in a couple of pages.

If either of you feel you need more lubrication—and, believe us, you *always* want to keep it nice and slippery (have we driven this point into your skulls yet?)—your friendly neighborhood adult store should have plenty from which to choose. If you live in a town that doesn't even have a movie theater, that's probably not an option for you, but your local drugstore should have personal lubricants like K-Y right out there on the shelves in front of God and everyone. (We prefer to march right up and ask the pharmacist for it out loud. Sure, we could get it ourselves, but we want others to know we're getting laid.) If you're online, there are also tons of Web sites up to their tits in different kinds of lubes, lotions, joy jellies, and other amazing goop that some lucky schmuck gets paid to invent. Most gay male magazines (like the highly stylish and affordable *Instinct*) will have advertisements for lube, complete with phone numbers or, sometimes, order forms. Don't know why that is. Gay men, dicks, and lube—go figure. If you don't like one kind of lube because it dries out or tastes unpleasant or feels greasy or whatever, get another. In a free country the choice is yours! You can pick your politicians and you can choose your lube! (Besides, there's not much of a difference between the two: They're both used to fuck you.)

FORESKIN AND SEVEN YEARS AGO...

If he happens to be uncircumcised, you can use his foreskin as an additional form of lubricant. (And no, that doesn't mean his foreskin is a liquid, dummy. It's just an expression. Sheesh.) Remember our telling you how an uncut guy can just grab his dick and start jerking off because the foreskin slides so nicely? Once you put a lip lock on his uncut sex stick, you can use this to your advantage by allowing your mouth to move the skin up and down with your bobbing motions.

But when you really get down to business, you'll want to use a couple of fingers to pull the foreskin down to expose the head. That's because that is where most of the nerves reside that tell his brain that what you're doing feels damn good. The more neurons you fire off, the closer you are to being able to call him your bitch and get him to do whatever you so desire. Hell, he might even poison your wicked stepmother for ya if you're good enough.

GIVING HIM LOTS OF LIP

Your lips are used for a lot of great things. They help you speak. They

TAKE ME OUT TO THE BALL GAME

There are all sorts of things you can do with the cute little twins. You can tie 'em up all kinds of ways. The most standard way is to use a strap of leather with snaps made for the purpose, or a strip of leather, or some kind of tying material. No matter what way, it generally goes around the top of the scrotum, forcing the testes down away from the body. The tying is snug but not tight. The object is not to strangle them but to add an interesting sensation to whatever you're doing. Usually the part of the scrotum with the balls in it will be stretched taut. That opens them up to all the available textures and sucking we discussed earlier.

There are also ball separators: usually metal or leather doodads that you stick the testicles into and then into separate areas that hold them apart from each other, making each one available for the texture, sucking, etc. And you can do something different to each one at the same time.

Let us not forget ball stretchers, which is really a misnomer. What you're stretching is the scrotum. It's a leather cuff of varying lengths, usually with snaps. You put it around the top of the scrotum, snapping it into place. The ball stretcher pushes the nuts down to the bottom of the ball sac rather tightly, depending on the length of the ball stretcher you're using. Some guys have lots of scrotum to play with, so they use longer ball stretchers. It's a way of putting pressure on the testicles as well as gathering them tightly in one place for all the fun sensations you can cause them.

Some guys get into the constant tug on their scrotum achieved with ball weights. There are a couple of different kinds of these, the most popular called a parachute ball weight. It's composed of a somewhat cone-shaped piece at the top, usually leather, through which the testicles can be pushed. It's then tightened snugly around the top of allow you to kiss your mate and make them swoon with desire. Julia Roberts and Angelina Jolie have used theirs to nab Oscars. (What, you thought it was their acting ability?) Lips are also crucial to pickling his pecker. Basically, you'll want to purse your lips so you establish solid contact each time that penis slides on through. You can vary the ways you do that so that your lips don't get too tired. A very light pucker has a nice feel too, and is an interesting change from a firm lip lock,

the scrotum. From the sides of the leather top are small chains that come together a few inches below the balls in a parachute shape, hence its name. Weights are hung from where the chains come together. The more weights, the more tug on the scrotum and balls.

What you've most likely seen in porno are the guys wearing cock rings. These are made typically of metal, leather, rubber, or neoprene. While still flaccid, you stick the penis and testicles through it. When the dick gets erect, it makes the cock ring tight around the base of the penis and the balls. A cock ring is used to help maintain the erection by constricting blood flow from the penis. Blood comes in, can't get out, dick stays hard. Simple as that. The problem can arise when the cock ring is so tight that it can't go down even after ejaculation. Blood can't leave, dick stays hard, owner goes to emergency room to have cock ring cut off before it causes gangrene. If

you're going to play with a cock ring, we suggest an adjustable one, like the leather cock rings made with snaps for varying sizes. Of course, you can achieve the same effect by tying leather straps or rope around the cock and balls. Just be sure to open it up from time to time.

There are plenty of other delightful things that can go on with this area, including S/M (sado-masochism) and CBT (cock-and-ball torture). These are perfectly acceptable areas to explore both as a couple and individually, but they have a much more specialized focus than the basic blow job we're going for here. You may have noticed that we often say "Experiment with what works for you." That's not because we're lazy but because you'll discover differ-ent things affect different people in very different ways. When it comes to practices from S/M to tantric sex, suffice to say, you'll need to do your own exploring.

which has charms of its own. Why don't you try them both on your finger? Go ahead, we'll wait.

Fun, huh?

Another variation is to cover your teeth with your lips—you know, like you do when you imitate your grandpa without his dentures. In fact, we have a theory that this is why some younger fellas go for older guys (or gals): You don't have to worry about covering up your teeth at all if you don't have any! Let's just say that tearing up his member isn't the biggest turn-on, so try to avoid scraping his tadger with your teeth.

SPEAKING IN TONGUES

Creating some suction can help maintain lip-to-love-muscle contact. A bonus is that it also allows the tongue to get into the act. You control the amount of suction by tongue placement and by letting his withdrawal action (the part of the motion with the dick pulling out) create a vacuum in your mouth. That's what pulls the tongue into close contact with his penis for friction. It also pulls the soft palate down for contact along the top of his cock. Try doing that on your finger too. We're serious. If there are people around, fuck 'em, let 'em stare.

Let's talk about that tongue. Did you know that, ounce for ounce, it's the strongest and most developed muscle in the body? Think of how deft you've become making it fly all around your mouth as you talk, especially with all the gossip *you* spew. What an amazing tool your tongue is! And now you get to use your tool on his tool. It makes even you femme girls and queeny queens sound butch. There's licking, flicking, fluttering, using the tip, using the whole broad expanse, poking with it hardened or with it soft, back and forth, up and down, sensuously swirling, exploring—whew! We're getting hot and bothered just thinking about it!

Right. Now you may be wondering how much suction is the right amount of suction. Sorry, but you're going to have to find that out for yourself. Not because we don't feel like telling you but because it's going to be different for each boy you boff. Besides, despite our best efforts and what you've no doubt read about us on bathroom walls, the chances that we've sucked the very guy you're kneeling in front of are pretty slim. The basic rule is that the more sensitive he is, the less suction you need; the less sensitive he is, the more force you can employ. Size or shape of the penis doesn't matter here. If he's really big, he's not used to getting it all in anyone's mouth anyway, so just concentrate on what you can get in, use a hand for the rest, and be glad that the head is the most sensitive part.

A SHOW OF HANDS

You also get to use your hands during a blow job, although, like riding a bike, it'll impress your mother if you don't have to. (Look Ma, no hands!) You'll usually be concentrating on the head of the penis and the adjacent part of the shaft with your mouth. Feel free to use your hand(s) to work on the base of his dick. Throwing your hands into the mix is not cheating; it's giving him more stimulation in addition to your luscious lips. And trust us, as long as his dick is getting stimulated, he's not going to complain. Again, just make sure your hand is nicely lubricated, whether with spit or lube. Coordinate your hand strokes with your back-and-forth head motion and it will feel great to him! You can even let your hand fully take over for a bit while you lick or suck his balls. Or just use your hand to keep stimulating him while your mouth takes a little breather or you shift positions. As far as oral sex goes, the Universe gave us hands so we could cope with lip and jaw fatigue. Hey, that's our theory and we're sticking with it!

But having hands isn't an excuse to stop blowing him. As men, we would like to ask that you not switch over to just giving a hand job here. Yes, he'll shoot his load, but a hand

500,000

number of men who get vasectomies each year.

$750

approx. cost of a vasectomy

job just doesn't feel as wonderful (or intimate) as the blow job you came here to learn how to do. Besides, while men are more than capable of giving themselves hand jobs, if autofellatio (blowing yourself) were as prevalent, men wouldn't leave the house and women would run the world. So while using the hands for a breather or as an adjunct to your cock sucking is fine and dandy, bailing out on the BJ in favor of jerking him off is cheating him out of the wonderful experience you're learning how to provide. Besides, you haven't read this far to learn how to give hand jobs, now, have you?

THIS REALLY BITES

By now you've probably figured out that for a blow job, pretty much anything goes in terms of oral activity. That's basically true—except for one thing: teeth! No teeth, please! If you are scraping his penis with your teeth, you are ruining the experience for everyone. It hurts the hell outta him and it's a real wood kill. Not only that, but if you break the skin, you are raising health issues for both of you, including hepatitis and HIV. Plus, it really hurts! So how do you avoid that?

First, think preemptively. Be aware of where your teeth are in relation to the boy banana you're about to take in your mouth. Look at it and imagine how it's going to fit in your mouth. Is it impossibly wide at the base? Keep that in mind when you get down there. Deep-throating him may be out of the question if your teeth are in the way of that. There's no shame in this, by the way.

If he's not that wide, you may only need to be aware of your front teeth (upper and lower) as you bob on his knob. It's a crazy-making thing to be getting an otherwise great blow job except that with every downstroke the front teeth scrape like hell. We men don't want to stop the blow job because what feels good feels *so-o-o* good, but that scrape scrape scrape is hurting like hell! Just be aware, that's all we're asking.

In the area of deliberate biting, there can be love nibbles—

extremely light and *careful* nibbles—but only when you're fully concentrating on the nibbling at hand and not while you're otherwise mentally engaged in actively sucking him off. And when you *are* actively sucking, pay attention while you're going up and down on his dick. Learn to let his penis in and out easily without hitting your teeth. More math: dick + teeth = bad, OK? This is very, very important, so fuck the split infinitive: *Learn to not do this!*

THAT UP-AND-DOWN THANG

The blow job requires your mouth going from the tip of his dick, toward his body, and back again. Repeatedly. Just what is the best way of achieving that? Well, everybody has their preferred methods, much of it depending on what position they're in. Let's start with the most basic on-your-knees position:

1. You can move your head back and forth at your neck. This is good for bobbing on his dick at a relatively rapid rate but can be used for a slower rate as well.

2. You can move back and forth bending at your chest. This gives you a medium pace, but again, this can be done at a slower rate as well.

3. You can also do it bending at your waist. This will necessarily give you the slowest pace because it involves moving your entire torso with each stroke.

If you practice these methods, you'll find that each uses different sets of muscles. This is good to know when one set begins to tire. One of the reasons people cite for not wanting to slurp on the salami is that they find the repetitive motion tiring. Whether it's in the lips, jaw, neck, or whatever, if you start getting fatigued, vary what you're doing. Oh, and keep sucking.

Of course, if you can coordinate it with your partner, he can give your neck a rest by doing the thrusting himself—if he can control that without jamming his rod in deeper than you want to take. Yeah, that'll happen. If he's lying down and you're bending over him, whether from the side or from on top of him, you can support your torso with your elbows and bob with your neck. When you get bored with that, support yourself with your arms: That way you can bend at your chest, like doing a mini push-up, and use those muscles. You'll be pleasing your man and working your pecs out all in one. You may never have to go to the gym again.

Or you can even use your arms to lift yourself up and down on his cock. If you're on your side, you can use one arm in the same way. You get the idea. When you get tired, simply switch to something else, and keep doing that until you've finished him off.

OVERSTIMULATION

Because certain areas have so many erotic nerve endings, it is possible to overload them. He may indicate this by pulling back and saying he needs a little rest. It might even manifest itself as an almost painful reaction. Don't stress over this. It merely means you've sent so many happy messages from so many tingled nerve endings that his brain can't handle it and needs to temporarily shut down the affected area. Usually all that's needed is a moment or two for him to recover.

If he suddenly pulls away and you're unsure what that's about, feel free to ask, "Too much?" Find out what activity on what area caused the overload, and when activities resume, do what you ordinarily would, just go at that area with a bit of a lighter touch.

TECHNIQUE #1: GETTING THERE IS HALF THE FUN

OK, so this isn't exactly a dick lesson per se. But it's a helluva great lead-in. When sex is on the menu, guys go immediately for their dicks. There are two lessons to be gleaned from this. The first one is that guys haven't learned, as women have always known, that the best sex is not just about what's between the legs. It helps to take the long way down by first arousing him everywhere you can think of before you get to the gonads. Nibble his neck, stroke his stomach, tongue his torso, gnaw his, um, gnipples. It's entirely possible, even probable, that the poor sap has never fully explored his body, so show him where his erogenous zones are. Inside the elbow, the small of his back, his wrist and fingers, behind the knee, all over his ears, his manly butt, his furry inner thigh, his tight little anus, the bottoms of his feet, his nuts, and who-knows-what other places you will discover for him?

The other lesson is that this "dick first and only" mentality should tell you just how important the penis is to a man—as if sports car ads and ESPN hadn't clued you in. A major reason it's this important is that his cock is covered with tingly little nerve endings all tied to the erotic region in the brain. You can use this to your advantage by taking your…own…sweet…time…getting there. Slo-o-owly getting closer and closer to his cock. The more you caress and stroke him elsewhere, the more buildup you are creating for him. Do your job well and he could be begging for you to join the groin now, now, NOW! But don't do it, honey. Not until you're good and ready. Let him suffer. Deliciously, but suffer nonetheless. Because when you finally do arrive at the center of his world, he is going to be so ready for it that your job is going to be a breeze. Now then, since breezes blow and so will you, let's get down to some time-tested techniques.

TECHNIQUE #2: LICKING THE LOVE STICK

He wants his dick in your mouth. Fine, just not yet. Lick it first. Start with your tongue under the back of his balls. Gently flicking your tongue back and forth, go over his balls toward the front to the base of his penis, then give him a nice, slow lick along the bottom of the shaft all the way to the tip. Do this several times. Feel free to vary the way you lick. For instance, you might consider the back-and-forth tongue flicker along the bottom of the shaft or use small upward licks as you move from the base to the tip. Don't forget to give the frenulum a special lapping. Try slowing down that back-and-forth tongue movement to cover the entire underside of his dick. Invent your own tongue motions as you notice what pleases him most. Lick along the sides of his cock. Use your lips along it as if you were playing a harmonica. Heck, hum along if you like. The vibration will add to the stimulation.

After he's had enough of that, lick just the head of his penis for a bit. When you think he's ready, take only the head in your mouth. Swirl your tongue around it, making sure to lick the coronal ridge and the friendly frenulum. Take your time; you don't have to be anywhere, do you? Add a little suction as you swirl that tongue, slowly increasing said suction. Begin taking the head in and out of your mouth. After doing that a dozen or so times, take a little bit more of his cock—but only a little more—in your mouth each time. When you have gotten to where you are taking all of it you can, vary the sucking with the licking, leaving out no part of his dick but concentrating on the head.

TECHNIQUE #3: HEAD GAMES

Suck up and down only on the tip of his glans. Do it actively so the intensity will build. Then suck on only the top half of it for a while. Then suck on it like that all the way down to the corona—but not past it. After a while, suck down over the corona. Are you getting the picture? You are teasing him by only taking a very specific—and limited—part of him into your mouth at an intense activity level. Then you keep increasing how much you take step-by-step. Slo-o-owly. It's agonizingly delicious!

CHEAP TRICKS

That's tricks to use, not invite over, although many of them give excellent head. Um, so we're told. Anyway, here's a couple of fun alternatives it couldn't hurt to try:

TEMP JOB. We've talked about friction, sensitivity, lubrication, and technique. Try altering the temperature. Suck on an ice cube and then go down on him. That will provide him with a very interesting experience. You can alternate by taking a slurp of a hot (not too hot, though!) liquid before sucking on him. If it's a small enough piece of ice and his penis is the right size, try sucking him with the ice in your mouth at the same time. For some of us, that ice thing is like getting head from the dead, but we say try it. It's worth it if it stands a chance of making him your love slave.

MINT CONDITION. You can also increase his sensitivity while giving a new cooling sensation with mints. Pop a couple of heavy-duty mints in your mouth before

2%
of gay men have a genital piercing.

going down. The thing that gives the minty taste and cool, refreshing feeling is oil of some kind, usually peppermint, wintergreen, or clove. That oil is actually an irritant, which is what causes the increased sensitivity.

MORE LUBE! There are lubricants out there that have similar oils in them that will do the same thing. There are also lubricants that actually warm up when you blow on them, which is an interesting sensation. Our feeling about all of these things is, what the hell, give it a go! Unless you try new things, you'll never learn what it takes to rock your world.

EXTRA, EXTRA, READ ALL ABOUT IT!

Your lips, tongue, and soft palate all have a certain texture. Add other textures. You're covered with all kinds of them: hair, skin, stubble, fingernails. And the hair on your head is different from the hair on your arm or face. Likewise, the skin on your cheek is going to be a different texture than the skin on your hand. You can use these textures on and off to create interesting sensations on his dick, scrotum, inner thighs, and perineum. Ever so gently rake your fingernails through his pubic hair. Gather up his balls and gently let him feel the stubble on your chin or the silkiness of your hair. As long as you're eating him, learn to look at your body as a menu of possibilities!

BITE ME

Remember back there where we told you, "Be careful, don't bite— ever!" and then beat you over the head with that? Well, forget it.

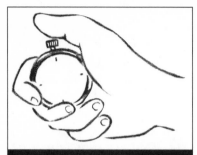

COME IN 60 SECONDS!

We all know there will come a day when you really don't have the time to lavish all the lovingly lingering and luscious care on your man that we've been learning. Maybe you're blowing him in the airplane lavatory and people are beating on the door. Or your husband could come downstairs at any moment. Or you've sobered up and want him out of your apartment.

Here's how ya do it: Start sucking and suck like mad. Go! Go! The clock is ticking! Try out two or three sucking techniques in a row right off the bat. Quickly pick the one that gets the best response and *keep at it*. Get a couple of things going at the same time, like tugging on his ball sac or fingering his asshole while you're blowing him—anything that makes him weak in the knees. Make the noises and eye contact if you can and if it works, but *do not stop sucking him*. If your lips get tired, use the hand-assisted method discussed earlier. The trick is to give his genitals so much sensation that his dick can't help but shoot. Keep sucking him! Here it comes! Yes! Yes! Oh, God, yes!

Why? Because we made our point, and now we want to take the whole teeth thing to another level and give you a fun technique you may want to use. See, nobody wants teeth getting in the way of a blow job, but once you understand the concept of always being aware of where your teeth are in relation to his dick, you can actually use your chompers.

Think of the many features of a Swiss army knife. If you know how to use all the different components (say, the corkscrew), it can give pleasure by opening a nice bottle of wine. If you just wave that corkscrew around willy-nilly, though, you can do some real damage. It's a matter of knowing your instrument, which for our purposes is your mouth. One of the many features of your mouth is teeth. Used properly and skillfully, they can give pleasure. Used carelessly, you'll never get that second date.

So how do you use your teeth? Very carefully.

You want to give him the sensation of nibbling first. *Not*

biting but gently nibbling. Where you nibble is up to you. The underside of the penis, all over the foreskin, around the head, along the side like an ear of delicate corn. Note the reaction you get in various places. The nibble on a thin bit of skin along the dick is going to feel very different from the nibble up and down the shaft with the head in your mouth. Don't be limited to just the cock, either. Inner thigh, pubic area, perenium—go exploring. You may have noticed one area we haven't mentioned. Hmm, what could that be?

Bite My Balls

Or rather, don't. Remember that the testicles themselves are delicate and easily hurt. You don't need to be chewing on them. But you *can* nibble on his scrotum. Bear in mind that sac is filled with epididymis plumbing too, and that needs to be avoided as well. You'll want to concentrate on only nibbling on the skin that encases all that noise. Don't be afraid of doing that, because it can feel very, very nice. We merely want you to be respectful of the contents. As with any technique you try, always pay attention to the reception it gets. If it's positive, continue. If it ain't, move on to something else that's fun.

Going to Town

Assuming the response to the nibbling is positive, you may want to move up from the nibble to the light gnaw as you munch on his manhood. Take it slower than slow as you work your way up on the teeth-pressure-to-skin scale, constantly checking in on how he's taking it. If the gnaw works out, try a gentle nip or two. Tug on that foreskin or even his scraggly scrotum. Always, always, always be aware of how each bite is received, and the moment it's no longer pleasant for him, be ready to ease off. Doing this, you can safely find out his limits and give him yet another sensory delight on his danglies.

PLAYING FOR TIME: DELAY TACTICS

Since he's a male conditioned by a goal-oriented society, your man probably wants to come now. You could do that if, say, your pastor is coming over in 20 minutes and he's not particularly open-minded about joining in. Or you could bring him (your man, not the pastor) to the edge a couple of times before you let him explode. The longer you make him wait, the more intense his orgasm is going to be. And *then* you can start on the pastor.

You can tell when a man's getting ready to ejaculate by, among other things, the tension in his muscles, the sounds he's making, and by his testicles withdrawing into his body. When this happens and you want to hold him back, there are a few easy ways to do it.

Delay Tactic #1: Controlling the Balls

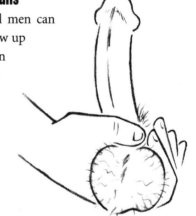

Here's a fun fact: Before almost all men can ejaculate, their balls have to withdraw up into or close to their body. You can postpone his orgasm by keeping his balls gently pulled away from his body. Now, you have to remember our little talk earlier about how sensitive the nuts can be and how that varies from man to man, but if you can make an "O" with your forefinger and thumb around the top of his scrotum and keep those guys from getting up there, you can hold up his coming pretty much as long as you want, no matter what you're doing to his dick.

Delay Technique #2: The Penis Pinch

Just before he goes over the edge, gently but firmly take the head of his dick between your forefinger and thumb, and press. Hold it for a few seconds until you feel the moment pass. He will most likely maintain his erection too, so it's not like you'll have to start over from scratch.

If you misjudge how close he is and he begins to come, let go! If you keep the head pinched and the urethra clamped shut while semen is trying to spurt out, the pressure can cause a rupture in the urethra. Ruptures usually don't feel good. Even a tiny one can mix a little blood in his semen, which will freak him out majorly. Skip the drama: If he starts to come, let him. Hell, at that point you want to egg him on anyway. Start sucking away if you're OK with that or beating him off. Enjoy the fireworks however they occur.

Delay Technique #3: Spread 'Em!

Many men have a more difficult time coming if their legs are spread widely apart. Oh, they'll want to come, they'll ache for it. But it'll take longer to happen if you can keep his legs apart.

Delay Technique #4: Blowing Hot and Cold

For this one to work, he can't be right there on the edge, just very close to it. When you sense he's getting close, stop sucking and blow cold air on his penis. That does two things: It's a complete stop of the friction your mouth and/or hands were providing, and the sudden chill is such a different sensation that it helps break up the chain of events leading to shooting sperm.

77

THINGS MOMMA NEVER TOLD YOU ABOUT SUCKING COCK

1. Blow your nose first. You gotta be able to breathe, right?

2. Get comfortable. You're gonna be there awhile, so don't get in some position that's gonna give you a cramp in five minutes.

3. Make eye contact. Men are aroused visually. Most enjoy looking down and seeing someone sucking on their giant, throbbing, virile, monster cock. Whatever. They dig it. Use it. And if he's not into that, just go about your business.

4. Make noises. Most men enjoy thinking that you're getting off on having their giant, throbbing, blah blah blah in your mouth, so make "yummy" sounds. You know: "Oh, yeah!" on the upstroke and "Mmmm!" on the down. Making humming noises also gives off vibrations that can feel very nice. (Why do you think they call it a hummer?) Some men enjoy the slobbery sucking sounds of having their dicks sliding in, out, and all around in your mouth, so don't be shy.

5. Have a repertoire. Don't be just a one-trick pony. So you're great at deep-throating, but there's a lot of other stuff you could and should be doing. Besides, when one activity starts to, uh, suck, or stops working, or becomes a bore or even a chore, you'll want to have plenty of other tricks up your sleeve to keep the party going. Learn what we've given you and be ready to mix and match. Ideally, you should become so good at this, you'll come up with some variations and specialties of your own and write your own damn book.

6. Review chapter 3. Because there are plenty of other things you can be doing to him with other parts of your body while your mouth is busy. Don't forget to use them!

6
OPERATION DEEP-THROAT

This is the technique everybody wants to know about: Is it actually possible to cram an entire big dick down your throat without gagging? Just how do you wrap your lips around his rod all the way down to the root? The answer is yes, and we'll tell you all about it. Later.

Because first you need to understand exactly what's going on in your gullet when this is happening. Go find a mirror and look at yourself with your mouth open. This is what you look like when you're sleeping, which is pretty awful, but get over it. OK, looking inside, there's your mouth of course, but what is that? Well, it's the part from the lips, past the teeth—including, along the roof, the hard palate and the soft palate to the back of your tongue. All of this is called the oral cavity. If we use the uvula (that little hangsy-downsy thing in the back) as a landmark, basically anything in front of that is the mouth, and behind it as far as you can see is the area known as the fauces. From where your throat turns downward is this whole other area called the pharynx, starting from about where you can no longer see to down around your vocal cords. It's where your windpipe (trachea) and the esophagus begin. About now you're thinking, *Yeah, so who gives a shit?* You do, honey, because this is where that long dick goes when you're deep-throating. This is prime choking territory, and you need to know the mechanics in order to control it. So shut the fuck up and keep reading.

CAN YOU TAKE IT?

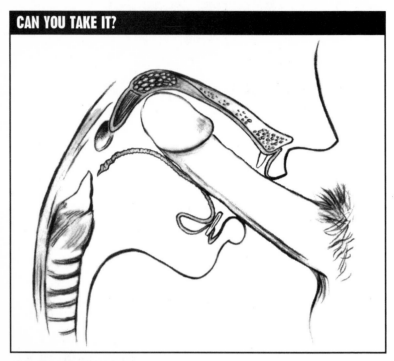

OF EPI- PROPORTIONS

The epiglottis is a flap of cartilage at the very back of your throat in the pharynx that normally rests in a somewhat upright position so air can go from your mouth or nose into your windpipe (trachea) and to your lungs. Or lung, if you've lost one to smoking. Ew. Anyway, when you swallow—and deep-throating counts as that—the epiglottis is pushed down to cover the trachea so food (or whatever) is directed toward your esophagus and stomachward. That's why you can't breathe when you're deep-throating. Duh. And, yes, there'll be more about breathing later on.

YE OLDE GAG REFLEX

You gag for a reason. And not just because he hasn't washed his nuts in a week. It's the body's defense against foreign thingamajigs from the pharynx and oral cavity. Your body tries to expel that object by dysphagia (gagging) so you can breathe. If you gag hard enough, it triggers a vomit response, which is the body expelling stomach contents in order to wash whatever's blocking the air passage out of the way. Not pretty, but it's a vital function that, under normal circumstances, is there to help keep you alive.

Clinicians use the gag reflex as a measure of how well a patient's ninth cranial nerve is functioning. (That's the glossopharyngeal nerve, for those of you who date nerds and want to impress them.) If the patient has a lousy gag reflex, it could mean food and fluids are going down his trachea, and that is bad. That's why having a healthy gag reflex is, as Martha would say, a good thing.

For our purposes, though, what we want to do is get around that reflex. We're going to teach you the three ways of doing that—of tricking that pesky ninth cranial nerve into shutting up and going along for the ride.

WANTING IT

So how do you accomplish this? First and foremost, you really have to want it. You can't be thinking about the laundry or what the hell that ugly mask from Pier 1 is doing on his wall. You can't be planning tomorrow's dinner party for eight or wondering why your uncle used to come in your room at night. Focus! *Want* it! We mean, "Oh, yeah, baby, give me your hot fucking dick—all the way—*now!*"

Why? Because sexual desire can make a person do amazing things. We could tell you stories about the guy who couldn't hold his breath for more than 20 seconds, yet when offered the opportunity to get his mouth around a hot guy's cock in the pool, he somehow stayed under for almost a minute and a half. Several times. Or the woman who never thought she could enjoy anal sex until one day she met an

.07

thickness, in millimeters, of the average condom

autumn

the most arousing time of year for a man; hormone levels peak.

amazingly sexy man and discovered she had no idea what she'd been missing. We could tell you plenty of other stories like this, but if you think about it, you probably have a few of your own. Take a moment right now and think about the last time you were so horny-sex-crazed that you surprised, maybe even shocked, yourself with what you did. Draw on that experience. Remember what it was like to be so turned on, you felt there was nothing you couldn't—or wouldn't—do in that moment. Now mentally put yourself there again. Oh, yeah!

The biggest sexual organ is the brain, baby. Use it. Get your mind around the idea that chowing down on this dick is the sexiest, most exciting thing you've ever done. Because if you're truly hot for it, that's half the gag reflex battle right there. Just remember to come up for air!

TAKING IT

Now that you've mentally worked yourself into a frenzy ready to suck his throbbing cock right down to the root, let's deal with the physical. It's time to use your knowledge of how the mouth, fauces, and pharynx are put together, because it is imperative that you align his dick with your throat. Remember, your throat curves down, so if he curves up, that ain't gonna work—at least not until you shift, say, into a sixty-nine–type position. That way, the curve of your throat now matches his curve. If he curves to the left or right, adjust yourself accordingly. If he curves down when hard, well, isn't he Mr. Convenient?

And what if he's a straight-pointer? In that case, you'll need to compensate a little differently, but it's not a big deal. See, straight, curved or whatever, you're basically doing a sword-swallowing act. When the guy at the circus puts the straight sword down his gullet, what does he do first? He aligns his mouth with his throat by tilting his head back so the blade can go straight down. That's what you get to do. He needs to understand this too. (Um, your partner, not the Great Swallowini.) If lover boy is expecting you to deep-throat him and he's not allowing you to get in a position where you can take it, he's just going to be pounding away at the back of your throat. It's like trying to jam a pencil down an elbow pipe joint. *Muy* unpleasant. Get yourself in a position where you can bend your head back to make a clear path for his pushy penis. And get him to work with you, damn it!

PRACTICING IT

The rest of it is practice, my dears, practice. You need to get that goofy ol' glossopharyngeal nerve used to having something stimulating it without it getting its panties in a wad and going to the next step—making you gag. The way to do that is with a regimen of regular, controlled stimulation to that area. The key word here being *controlled.*

Try it on a banana. Peel it first. Then slowly go down on it, seeing how far back on your tongue you can take the banana before you feel your gag reflex starting to kick in. If you can, hold the banana where it is. Concentrate on relaxing, keeping your throat open, and not gagging. See if you can count to 10. Then slide the banana out. Take a deep breath. And try it again. See if you can count a little higher than you did before. Practice that for a while. (Note: This isn't a competition, so don't rush it. When we say *a while,* it could mean a few minutes, a period of days, or even weeks. Go at your own pace.)

After you feel more confident with that, see if you can take the banana a little farther into your throat. Each time you feel the gag reflex start, stop pushing the banana, hold it there, and count like you did in the previous paragraph. Over time, you can use this method to take more and more of the banana. You may even want to try it out on an actual dick. Go for it. You might just surprise yourself. Just don't push yourself too hard, because vomiting in his crotch is a turnoff for most men. If you do gag, simply pull back—and remember, this is a learning process. You're teaching your throat not to do what it ordinarily would do to protect you from choking on food. It's very likely that when you do try this with an actual cock, you'll find you can take more than you thought because of the excitement of the moment.

If performance anxiety kicks in for you, or some other concern keeps you from taking as much as you wanted or thought you could, don't let it bother you. Remember all the other fun things we've gone over in this book that'll make him quite happy.

Take these oral practices in baby steps. You don't have to get this down by tonight. With practice and time you can usually overcome at least some of that reflex. Go at your own pace and work on it every chance you get. This is one skill, though, you might not want to practice at the food court. Unless, of course, you're trying to impress that hot busboy.

IT'S IN THE AIR

Yes, Virginia, you do need air. When you had his penis only in your mouth, you were able to breathe through your nose and the air could get to your lungs because the epiglottis was open. With a dick down

12.5

average age a man starts producing sperm

your throat, your epiglottis is going to close off your windpipe. No air can get down to your lungs. Nope, not gonna happen. Don't even try to inhale or exhale.

Now, just because we've been practicing getting that cock all the way down our throat doesn't mean that coming up for air is "failure." On the contrary, passing out from lack of oxygen would be failure. Having someone who was sucking your dick suddenly collapse and need a 911 call does nothing to help maintain an erection, either. And remember, if it happens, you'll most likely be naked and not at your best when the handsome

EMTs arrive. So breathe, honey, breathe. We'll even tell you why it's a stimulating thing for your man.

See, as good as it feels to your man to be totally inside you, it's going to feel great going inside you again after you've pulled back for a breath of air and then gone back down on him. Remember, the going-in and going-out is what gives so much sensation. And when you do pull back, you don't have to go completely down on him again right away. You can keep sucking on the head and part of the shaft while you catch your breath. Go back to deep-throating him only when you are ready to return to it. Each time you do return, he'll be immensely grateful all over again.

So now you know the four big secrets to deep-throating:

1. Really, really want it.

2. Make your head position match the direction of his dick.

3. Practice, practice, practice.

4. Breathe!

OTHER POINTERS

Pay attention to how you are feeling when taking his dick down your throat. If you sense a gag coming on that you can't suppress, back off immediately! When you are going down on his dick with the intention of deep-throating him, it can help to inhale. Obviously, once it gets past a certain point, you can't breathe, but until then, inhale. Beyond that point, consider using some creative visualization to help get past that gag reflex. For instance, imagine your throat opening up like a snake's, or visualize a train entering a tunnel where there is plenty of room for it. Come up with an image that works for you.

He may want to cram his whole rod down your gullet. You may or may not want him to do that. Always remember: YOU ARE IN CHARGE. As Samantha said on *Sex and the City,* "You may be down on your knees, but you've got him by the balls." You take only as much of his cock into your mouth as you can or wish to take. Got it? There are all sorts of ways to please him orally without necessarily deep-throating him, so don't let yourself be forced into anything you don't feel comfortable doing.

It may happen that you run into a dick you just can't take because it's too damn fat, curved, long, or whatever. The mere fact that you tried shows that you're game. There's no dishonor in deciding after the attempt that it's not gonna work. There is no man alive who will not experience smug pride in being "too big." You can always use the other techniques you've learned to give him a memorable blow job.

It should be pointed out that some people are simply not going to be able to control their gag reflex. For these few people, no amount of practice and desire is going to make that gosh-darn glossopharyngeal nerve cooperate. If you should turn out to be one of these folks, you need to know that you don't suck at sucking. On the contrary, you possess a much more powerful ninth cranial nerve than the rest of us, and we secretly hate you for it. With a gag reflex as healthy and active as yours, you'll never die of choking like the rest of us could. So don't worry about it. The least you could do, though, is learn the Heimlich maneuver for when one of us needs it.

WHY YOU WANT TO DO THIS

You wouldn't have read this far unless you were intensely interested in making the guy you've got as happy as a pothead in Amsterdam. We love that about you. So we're going to tell you exactly why else you want to try going for it.

1. It's great for your reputation.
2. It's a terrific ego thing to know you can take him.
3. It's very sexy having him—all of him—in your mouth.
4. It's very exciting for him.
5. And it's just way fuckin' hot, OK?

As we stated at the outset, having a gag reflex is natural. But by practicing the exercises in this chapter and concentrating on your goal, you can learn how to suppress it—if not entirely, at least partially. And on behalf of the 49% of the world's population who sport woodies and XY chromosomes: THANK YOU, THANK YOU, THANK YOU!

7

POLE POSITIONS

And we keep going, and going, and... Yes, there is even more for you sexy suckers to learn. Hmm, maybe *learn* isn't the best word to use. It sounds so clinical, huh? How about *absorb*? Nah, now it sounds like a feminine hygiene product. Anyway, rather than search for the right word to keep you reading, let's just jump right into this next chapter. If you peek ahead, you'll notice a lot of scandalous drawings, so you know this is going to be fun.

We've already gone over quite a few spicy tricks you can try on your man, so now it's time for you to get a bit more involved. Some of these may appear pretty basic, but if you mix 'em up with some of the techniques discussed in the last two chapters, along with location (which we'll discuss in chapter 9) or timing—well, let's just say your sex drive will probably run out of gas before you can try all these combos. So if we ever hear you complaining about how boring your nookie is, we officially give ourselves permission to come over and slap you. Got it? Good.

What else do you need to know? Well, nothing really. We've already given you an earful about how every guy is different and how important it is to go into this suckfest with a sense of fun. But we need to fill up this page in order for the book design to be all nice and neat, so we've got a humorous little story about one of our exes. He thought he was the *shit* at giving head, or so he told all of our friends. Well, one night while we were going at it, he started to...

WHAT'S 68 + 1?

Oh, maybe you'll get to hear the rest of that story later. Anyway, here's a classic position for giving head. As you learned in the deep-throating chapter, this one can be quite useful if you're looking to swallow him whole.

WHAT'S GOING ON? One of you lies on your back while the other climbs on top and faces the other direction. Basically, your crotches

should be in each other's faces. The person on top can maneuver more easily, so it's probably better for them to be giving head. Of course, for you gay boys, if you can simultaneously suck one another off, well, aren't you special? If the guy on the bottom can't really position himself correctly to give proper head, no worries. We're sure your partner won't mind if you lick his balls or rim him while he's taking care of your come cannon.

As for the ladies, this is an ideal position because your boyfriend (or husband, or fuck buddy) is essentially forced to give you oral pleasure. Not that he has to be forced. Anyway, from what most of the women said, it's best to be on top in this position. You have more control of how deep or fast you want to go, plus you can easily take a break every now and then, and lick his balls or whatever else is down there that catches your fancy.

WHY THIS POSITION WILL ROCK YOUR WORLD. You mean *besides* the fact that you're both naked and undulating on each other? Well, you're also receiving pleasure simultaneously. What's even better than getting your dick sucked? Getting your dick sucked while doing the same to your studly stud! For a lot of people, just having a stiff, throbbing cock in their mouths is hot in itself. Combine that sensation with getting rimmed or eaten out or blown yourself, and it doesn't take a genius to figure out that you're adding to the pleasure quotient. See, math *can* be fun!

HAVE A SEAT

You'll notice a theme running through this book: It doesn't matter where, when, or who might be watching, men will usually settle for just about any place for a hummer. However, what's more relaxing than sitting in your favorite chair while your honey varnishes your wood? Of course, try to refrain from watching TV over his or her head. It's considered rude.

WHAT'S GOING ON? He's sitting, you're sucking. The key here is comfort, both for him and you. If the ground is hard or the carpet's giving you burns, kneel down on a pillow or cushion of some sort. While it may be difficult to play with his balls or ass in this position, you'll be a lot closer to his chest and upper body, which you can rub your hand over and pinch or massage. **WHY THIS POSITION WILL ROCK YOUR WORLD.** He'll feel like a king, and you can really concentrate on his dick. What's more, if you both are comfortable (which is the point of this one), then you can both take your own sweet time.

STAND AND DELIVER

Another no-brainer, this approach is also great if you two want to have a blow job on the run. You know, quickies have their appeal too. If you're at some boring social function or in an elevator ride to

the 87th floor (just make sure there's no camera), all you have to do is whip it out and start sucking away. Really, the only thing that can keep this from being the most no-nonsense method is if the person on their knees has any hang-ups about swallowing. Seriously, where else are you going to put that stuff?

WHAT'S GOING ON? Have him stand—either freely, if you'd like him to have control, or against a wall, if you'd like to take command. You can just take his dick out, or pull his pants down enough to expose his tush. The latter allows you to grab and massage his butt while you suck him off. It can also help you to manage the speed and force of his thrusts because, yes, he *will* be thrusting.

WHY THIS POSITION WILL ROCK YOUR WORLD. Ever since you were little you've appreciated the thrill of possibly getting caught doing something you shouldn't. Well, except for all you Goody Two-shoes out there. (You're probably reading this book in some dark corner anyway.) There's also the sheer carnal energy that goes into something so basic. It's all about giving it good in a short period of time. If you take too long, either he'll get tired of standing or you'll get tired of kneeling. Plus, you can't keep the elevator alarm on forever, you know?

FROM DOWN UNDER

This is one of those positions that proves sex can be a workout. One of the great things about oral sex with guys is how forceful they can get. The person underneath will have to be pretty receptive in order to pull this one off.

WHAT'S GOING ON? The blower should lie down on a comfortable surface (we suggest a bed). The blowee hovers over them in a push-up position with their legs spread so they can control their movement. However, rather than move their whole body down like you would for a push-up, just thrust your midsection. The person on the bottom can either push or pull, depending on how fast they'd like to get it. Remember, it's not polite to talk with your mouth full.

WHY THIS POSITION WILL ROCK YOUR WORLD. For one, the person on top won't be able to stay poised above their partner for long, so every thrust has got to count. Also, how fuckin' hot is it to have a guy in a basic-training pose fucking your face? Way hot, we say.

ON THE SIDE

A variation of the classic sixty-nine above, this allows both partners equal access to each other's midsections. But what sets this apart is that it has the "double your pleasure, double your fun" aspect of sixty-nining mixed with the comfort you saw in "Have a Seat."

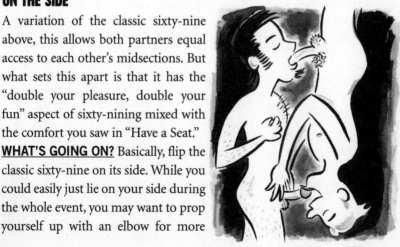

WHAT'S GOING ON? Basically, flip the classic sixty-nine on its side. While you could easily just lie on your side during the whole event, you may want to prop yourself up with an elbow for more leverage. Don't worry, because you still have one hand free to do whatever you need to do to make him shoot.

WHY THIS POSITION WILL ROCK YOUR WORLD. Simple. You can take your time, plus it allows you to explore his inner thighs and balls with your tongue and his butt with your free hand. Moreover, either

GO SUCK YOURSELF!

Ah yes, no doubt you've heard about the guy who slipped up and broke his neck trying to blow himself. What a way to meet your maker, but at least you can't say he didn't die not trying.

Autofellatio: a word that will immediately pique the interest of most guys because, whether they'd like to admit it, most of them have attempted to do it. Granted, most straight guys probably tried to suck themselves back in high school when they couldn't get one from their girlfriends and just about anything went, sexually speaking.

But even as grown-ups, a lot of gay guys are intrigued by the possibility of never needing to go out and pick up another man again. However, pulling up to the self-serve station is more elusive than you'd think. However, if you're determined to never go outside again, here's what you need to do:

1. LOSE WEIGHT. That's if you have a few extra pounds to shed: the tighter your tummy, the better to reel in your dick. Obviously, if you can't see your dick right now, the possibility of being able to reach it with your mouth is pretty, uh, slim.

2. FOCUS. As with deep-

throating, you've got to want it. No, you've *really* got to want it. If autofellatio is your goal, understand that it's going to take time to work up to the point where you can guarantee yourself a career in porn.

3. ARE YOU FLEXIBLE? If not, you're going to need to be. If you can't remember the last time you were able to bend over and touch your toes, don't fret. There are a handful of ways to go about getting limber so you can lick your lumber. One of them is yoga, which helps to not only stretch you out and make you more flexible, but it also teaches you discipline. Could autofellatio be one of the explanations for yoga's popularity? Hmmm...

4. PRACTICE. It takes patience and hard work to be able to run a 10K or swim laps in the pool without stopping. Same thing goes for this.

It also helps if you, surprise surprise, have a long dick, although if you're average or small in size, you'll be all that more determined at your yoga classes.

So what's the payoff for all this hard work? Well, besides from never needing to troll the bars, you will definitely be the life of the next party you attend.

one of you can control the movements: Either he can do the thrusting or you can suck away. Even better, if you can get into a decent rhythm, both of you should be sucking and (face) fucking.

ON A PEDESTAL

A more exhilarating (and involved) form of "Stand and Deliver." The only real requirement is that you find a surface your partner can stand on that gets his dick at eye level. You don't want to be bending down or standing on your tippy toes for this. Oh, and make sure whatever he's standing on can support his weight.

WHAT'S GOING ON? Your partner is standing above you, on a chair or sturdy table, or something else that puts his crotch right in your face. You're standing too, which takes the pressure off your knees and makes it easier for you to beat off or explore below his waist with your hands.

WHY THIS POSITION WILL ROCK YOUR WORLD. For the fella on the raised surface, it's kind of a rush to not be standing on solid ground. Also, it's always nice to be able to look down and see somebody licking your candy cane. For the person down below, you're able to keep

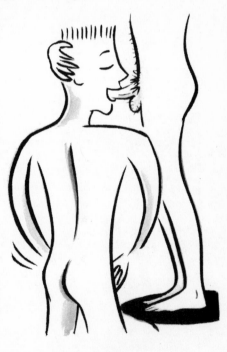

your balance better than you would on your knees, thus giving your hands more freedom. And it's always hot to look up and see how crazy you're driving your partner with the new tricks you picked up from this book.

VARY, VARY GOOD

These six positions will get you started, but we encourage you to come up with some variations of your own. Sometimes comfort is what you're looking for, while other times you'll be in the mood to try some more, uh, "acrobatic" moves. Whether you're sitting on the kitchen counter, lying upside down, or suspended from a sling, the more imaginative you are with your positioning, the more intense the experience. Just don't hurt yourself, OK?

8

THE BEST I EVER HAD

You didn't think you were going to get out of this without some good old-fashioned American smut, did you? Heaven forfend! Or maybe that's why you bought this trashy tumescence tome, as a sort of continuing education in cocksucking class. Whichever, we do our best to give you the honest, no-bullshit real deal, wrapped in plenty of foul-mouthed sarcasm and porn. We've already given you the academics, so let the filth begin!

GETTING YOU HOT AND BOTHERED

What's the point of learning how to improve (or start) your blow job career unless you think there's a pretty good chance it'll be fun, both for you, the giver, and for him, the receiver? That requires testimonials of great sex. Really, it does. We didn't want to stoop so low as to wallow in prurient salaciousness, but what can we do? If we don't get you excited about it, you may never go out and give it a go. You would have wasted all that time reading thus far and still not drop to your knees for the benefit of mankind. So we'll start with Clarice.

CLARICE'S TALE: FIRST-TIMER FELLATIO

Clarice is 40 and still fighting off the effects of a Catholic education. In her own words, it made her "a corporate vice president in the boardroom but a cold fish in the bedroom." She loved her husband,

Robert, but was sexually repressed, and after 10 years of marriage it had become a major issue at home.

"I had never considered having oral sex with my husband. My mother taught me it was disgusting and vile, and the nuns added 'sinful' to that. It took couples counseling, a sexual therapist, and half a bottle of Taitinger to get me to do the deed. It may sound foolish, but I suppose I expected his penis to taste, I don't know, foul or something. I was surprised to find it had no taste, like a finger or thumb. Robert is immaculate, so there was no unpleasant smell, either. There were really only textures. The different kind of skin around the testicles compared to his penis, plus the pubic hair and all of that. But I'm getting ahead of myself.

"When he became erect, I was a little frightened. I'd never been so close to it before. Well, not my head. So it looked enormous. And that's when things began to change for the better for me.

"My husband is very masculine. His looks, his movements, and God knows, the way he thinks. I've always found that maleness very attractive. Very exciting. And here in front of me was the single most overt physical demonstration of that. The masculine member, fully aroused. And then I thought, *I caused this!* and smiled. It was I making my husband's manhood stand at attention.

"I put my lips to it, it jumped! I had forgotten. I kissed the head. It jumped again. Already my mouth was causing him involuntary sexual response. I hadn't expected to feel powerful like that. I licked underneath the head. It jerked and Robert moaned. It was time I took him in my mouth.

74%

of men say they are OK with "that masculine smell," as long as it's not too overpowering.

"I opened and leaned forward, putting my lips on his penis about halfway down it. I was only touching him with my lips because I was worried about my teeth getting in the way. I moved back and forth like this a few times. I could feel all the small bumps and ridges caused by the blood vessels near the surface. It was very exciting learning this part of his body like this. From my husband's reaction, it was pretty exciting for him too. I continued moving back and forth, letting my tongue make contact, stroking him on the underside. I was surprised at how soft his penis felt in my mouth. You always hear the man say how hard he is—like a stone, like a club. But it wasn't. It was very firm and rigid—fully erect—but still smooth and soft.

"I found that I wanted to take more of him in my mouth. I leaned in farther and farther with each stroke, taking as much as I could. I only gagged once, but that told me my limit, so it didn't happen again. I became so aroused by the obvious pleasure it was giving Robert that I realized I wasn't just rubbing my lips and tongue against his penis, but I was actually sucking. Sucking because I desired it. I wanted it, him, in my mouth. I wanted his maleness in me. I had my left hand around the base of his penis, the better to keep it aimed toward my mouth. As my desire grew I could feel Robert starting to tremble. I cupped my right hand under his testicles. They were pulled up against his body. I lightly raked my fingernails forward over his tight scrotum, and he shouted he was coming.

"His semen spilled into my mouth, spurting against my tongue. My God, this was the essence of his masculinity shooting out of his penis, and it was in *my* mouth! I sucked on it greedily, wanting more, more, every drop of it. He was flopping like a fish but I stayed on him. I was sad at how quickly his erection faded. I felt like I had discovered an appetite I didn't know I had. I knew I would be doing this again.

"And I certainly have. I still enjoy it, but nothing can quite compare to the first time. That first time was about self-discovery and surprise. And while I can't say oral sex alone saved our marriage, it was, for us, a breakthrough. I continue to grow in confidence and skill, plus I've come up with a few other surprises for Robert. Still, when you discover something you really like, it's always the first time you remember fondest."

What Have We Learned? Clarice tells us:

1. Repression is bad news.
2. Repression can be overcome and replaced with positive views.
3. If you need to, don't be afraid to see a professional to do that.
4. Sexual preconceptions are often wrong.
5. Sucking a penis is not a terrible ordeal.
6. She discovered her own way to see oral sex as a turn-on.
7. She discovered her limits and wisely didn't push them.
8. She was open to surprising herself.
9. Billy Joel was right: Catholic girls grow up much too late.

GEORGE'S TALE: HOTEL DICK

George, 51, is a salesman for an airplane parts distributor. "I thought by my age I'd done it all and had it all. I was in Akron on business and wanted to get off. I had maybe an hour and a half between my last business meeting in the convention center and a client dinner in the hotel restaurant, so I wasn't even looking for anything, you know. I stopped in the bathroom in the lobby. I was at the urinal, you know, doing my business. This bellboy came in, said 'hi,' and started using the one next to me. There were only two, so it wasn't a big deal. But he was looking at me—well, at my *dick*. And then up at me. Very obvious. I'll admit, I liked the attention. Kinda skinny—wiry, I guess. Red hair. He must have been, I don't know, 20 maybe. Not usually my type. That young, they usually shoot in the first two minutes and call that a good time.

"Then he said two words: 'Can I?' I knew he wanted to suck me off. Well, I don't get that kind of offer from kids much, so I thought, *What the hey?* I turned so he could get a good view. By now I was hard. He looked around to make sure we were alone, then reached over. I thought maybe I'd been wrong, you know, and he just wanted to jerk me off. That was disappointing because, shit, I can do that myself. But he took his finger and touched it to the drop of piss at the end of my dick, then put the finger in his mouth. Oh, I wasn't wrong, this was a blow boy, all right. All I said was my room number, zipped up, and left.

"As soon as I got to my room, I took off my clothes. I left the door just barely ajar and pulled a chair around to face it. Sure enough, less than a minute later there's a knock, pushing the door open. He sees me sitting there, you know, naked with a hard-on. His eyes are about *this* big at that, but he slips inside and shuts the door quickly. He doesn't even get out of his bellboy uniform; he just falls to his knees.

29% of people say they only pay attention to the dick when giving head.

"Doesn't start blowing me right away. He rubs both hands over the inside of my legs. Ankles, knees, inside thigh. Bends his head and rubs his hair against my balls. Wavy red hair. It feels real good. Then he sticks his nose in that area under my balls and takes a real big sniff. He likes it. He starts licking that area. He continues up beside the ball sac where the leg joins. Both sides. And he's taking his time. It's a young kid and he's not going right for the dick. In fact, he goes back to the bottom for another big sniff, then starts in on my balls—gentle, flicking his tongue…I guess. I don't know, 'cause my head is back and my eyes are closed, 'cause it's just too damn good.

"He takes one ball in his mouth, rolls it around, working it in and out of his mouth with his tongue and lips. Then he does the other one. He takes a big breath and pulls both of 'em into his mouth. My dick's only normal size but my balls are pretty damn big, and he's got 'em both in his mouth. Both of 'em! I look down to see him looking up at me with these beautiful gray eyes. He just leans back, gentle like, tugging on my nuts. Then he glances at the tip of my dick, where precome's dangling, ready to drip. He lets go of my balls and runs his tongue up the bottom side of my dick up to the tip to get the precome. He pulls away, and there's a clear strand of fuck juice running from the tip of his tongue to my piss hole. That's so hot, my dick jerks

50%

of men prefer to tell their partner when they are about to come.

and another drop appears. That's it, he can't wait anymore, and the kid practically falls on my dick, sucking like crazy.

"Man, I don't know what the hell he was doing, but in 35 years of blow jobs I've never had anything like that. I've been blown by men, women, and in-between, but the combination of suction, the skin on his tongue, and sweet, warm slobber was better than anything I ever had. The feel of the sucking and the movement was unbelievable. This kid was fucking amazing. I could feel the jizz moving up from my balls, waiting for that place where you can't hold back anymore. And man, was I trying to hold back, 'cause this was too good to end. Up and down this kid went, like he had to have it or die. And he was gonna get it, because he suddenly started doing long, slow pulls on my dick with that amazing mouth of his and the jizz surged forward past any holding back. My body went stiff and I let out a howl like an animal. He could tell I was coming, so he pulled his head back and started pumping me with his hand. I shot over his shoulder three or four times before the jism slowed enough to just smear his uniform a couple of places. He shuddered and made a groan but kept pumping my dick until I had to pull away. Too sensitive, you know?

"I sat there trying to get my breath. Shit, man, I'm over 50 and I shot across the fucking room! Laughing, I looked down at the kid. He was breathing hard too, with this look on his face, all sweaty. 'You OK?' he asked. I laughed again. 'I'm OK,' I said, 'but you're fucking awesome!" He smiled. 'When do you get off?' I asked. 'I already did, sir,' he said as he stood up. There was a large wet stain on his uniform pants, a good seven inches from the center of his crotch. I asked if we could do this again. He said, 'Sure,' bent down, and started sucking my dick right there again! I told him I meant after my client dinner. And we did. In fact, I stayed three days longer than I needed just because of him and his amazing mouth. Funny thing was, it turned out he was a great kid even without the blow jobs—not that I ever needed to go without while he was around!"

What Have We Learned? George tells us:

1. Be open to possibilities as they present themselves.
2. Personal preconceptions are often wrong.
3. Not going right for the dick builds wonderful tension.
4. Playing with areas other than just the dick is fun.
5. Good suction creates slippery friction, which creates great sensations.
6. A good blow job can make you shoot like a younger man again.
7. People are more than blow jobs.
8. Lotsa spit is a good thing.
9. Men in uniform are hot.

BARRY'S TALE: TRUCK SUCK

Barry, 32, of Tacoma, Wash., made us change his name, age, *and* hometown for this book, so you know it's going to be good.

"My wife, Lena, was in the Navy, and while she was at sea for seven months she wrote that she'd been unfaithful. Like I hadn't been horny enough all that time, and she was fucking midshipmen? I was so mad I tore out of the house, got in my car, and drove around for hours. I realized I was on empty, so I pulled off at the first gas. It was a truck stop and it had a bar. Perfect, huh? By my third MGD I'd opened up to this truck driver. I mean big, like six-nine or 10, and 250 pounds easy. Had a goatee. Friendly, friendly face. With these eyes like you could trust him with anything. Name of Randy. Anyway, I'd been talking too long about my troubles and wife and all, so I start asking him about trucking. It's really fascinating. A lonely job but real interesting. He was telling me about his rig and all when outta the blue he asks if I'd like to see it. I felt this, this connection with him, so I said 'Yeah' and we headed out to the parking lot.

"He was parked on the far side of the lot and didn't have a load; it was just the rig. He kept it nice and it was real big, looked like it was real roomy. He climbed up and opened the door. Then he held his hand down for me. I coulda climbed up myself, but that big hand was reaching down for me, so I grabbed it. With one strong pull Randy had me up in the cab almost face-to-face. He smiled and said, 'Welcome to my home.' He showed me all the instruments and radios and whatnot. He said, 'This is where I work, but lemme show you where I live.' He climbed between the seats and pulled curtains back to reveal a bunk and a tiny living space with a little fridge and a hot plate. 'Have a seat,' he said. So I did. On the bunk. He sat down beside me and looked at me. My heart started going like a rabbit.

"See, I like women, but I've always also liked looking at men. Never did anything, just looked. And this man was looking at me. He leaned toward my face, and I instinctively pulled back. He looked deep in my eyes and ran his huge hand through my hair, around the back of my head. And gently pulled me toward him. He kissed me. He let go of my head and kissed me again. I didn't pull away. The next time, I kissed him.

26%
of men say they don't mind using a condom during oral sex.

"He slid off the bunk to his knees, massaging my thighs through the denim. He undid my belt and unzipped my fly, all the time looking right in my eyes. I must have looked nervous, because he said 'It's OK.' He took his shirt off. I didn't expect the tattoos or the hair. He tugged at my shirt and I took it off too. He pulled off my shoes, then tugged my pants down. I was hard and scared and horny as all get-out. Hell, I hadn't had sex with anyone but my right hand for seven months, how else should I be? I was shaking, but as Randy was kissing my stomach, I thought, *Fuck it, I'm so ready for this!*

"He had one hand around my ball sac, kind of pulling on it, while he went to work on my cock with his mouth. Every time I made a movement or gasped, he stopped and did whatever he was doing at that moment again, just to make sure he knew what caused the reaction. It was like he was taking notes on my prick. I know that made the difference. In college the girls would just go down on it, like 'How many licks does it take to get to the center of a Tootsie Pop,' and the faster they could do it and be done, the better. Lena was the same way. She'd attack it like a chore, like swabbing the deck or something. Randy was paying attention, really looking to see what got me going. Like, most guys are supersensitive on the head of their cock, but for me, it's the sides. He figured that out in about three strokes. Oh, and he kept playing with my balls the whole time. It felt like I had two people on me, one on my cock and the other on my nuts. Very hot. And his other hand was roaming all over me. Up tweaking my nipple, rubbing the back of my leg and thigh, massaging the area just above my cock. He wasn't just blowing me; he was *into* me.

"He reached up under my ass and pulled me forward so my butt was hanging off the bunk. Now his hand was groping my ass. He took his mouth off my cock so he could rub his head under my balls. He had them squeezed tight, just on the edge of hurting, and he rubbed his crew-cut hair over them. I'd never had that done to me, and I moaned. Instantly he stopped and asked, 'Does that hurt?'

"I think I said 'No-o-o!' because he laughed and did it some more. He rubbed his cheek against them. He needed a shave, and the dark stubble was unbearable but great at the same time. I had to make noise but I didn't want that to stop, so I kept shouting 'Yes!' Then, just as suddenly, the sandpaper torture stopped as he licked those tight balls with a wide, soft, soothing tongue. Jesus, that was great. He got into taking my balls in his mouth, then taking them out and blowing on them. Gave me the shivers. Then he'd take 'em back in his warm mouth. It was great every time.

"He paused just long enough to fumble in a box by the bed for some K-Y. He squirted some on his hand and used it to stroke the base of my cock while he sucked the head, giving lots of attention to the sides. He'd put a little on his other hand too, because I felt him smear it over my asshole. I wasn't sure about this, but I put my faith in Randy. He fingered around my asshole, doing a gentle little push in now and then. Meanwhile, his head was bobbing on the end of my cock while the other end was in his fist being pounded against my body in a coordinating rhythm. I was getting so close that I thought I was going to explode. Then he did it. He stuck one finger right up my ass. With a yell I blew like Old Faithful.

"Randy stood up, his pants around his knees, and in about half a dozen strokes whacked off, coming on my chest, stomach, and still jerking cock. I spent the night in Randy's truck cabin. And no, we didn't get any sleep.

"When Lena got back we divorced. Now and then I date women. Sometimes men, but as long as I'm getting alimony (you know, me the wounded party and all) I have to be careful about that. As for Randy, well, I have a CB radio in my car. I always know when he's coming. And he knows when I am."

What Have We Learned? Barry tells us:

1. Big emotions can make us open to other possibilities.
2. Paying attention to the responses you get makes all the difference.
3. Asking questions ("Does that hurt?") is a good thing.
4. Again, playing with other areas is way fun.
5. You have two hands and a mouth. Use them all.
6. Work those balls—gently. But work 'em.
7. Keep lube handy.
8. A little ass play can be stimulating.
9. Always keep in touch with nice people who give good head.
10. There's something about married men and truck stops.

MIMI'S TALE: CLASS ACT

Mimi is in her early 30s and, how shall we say it, a daughter of joy. "I'm a Vegas whore, honey."

"I started giving blow jobs at UNLV because it was easier than studying. Sucking off a professor was easy. Hell, half of them couldn't even get hard. They said they just wanted attention. Please! They wanted youth: mine. They think they're so smart and they never figured out it's not something you can suck out of people. If that were so, with all the sucking I've done I'd be a 5½-foot schlong.

"And sucking the younger ones, grad students who graded the exams? They were a piece of cake too. Five minutes and BANG! I got more A-pluses on my knees than I ever got with a pencil. One day I met this woman in a coffee shop off the Strip. I'll call her Judy. She was, like, five, six years older. We started talking. Turns out Judy's basically doing the same thing I am, only getting paid for it. She'd target the kids with expensive cars. Porsches, Jags. With that kind of money, daddy's never gonna notice Junior dropping a couple of hundred for hummers two or three times a week.

"But they don't do that for just any debutante blow job, see? You gotta take your time, make 'em beg. Then know how to deliver. Which, really, couldn't have been easier to do. I have a standard menu of things I do to feel a man out, so to speak. Whatever makes him jump, I do more. If there's a couple of things, I like to combine them. All I had to do was slow down and I could be leaving with something that'd help my bank account instead of just my GPA.

"Judy was moving downtown in a month or so, for the gamblers and conventions. So she introduces me to her campus guys. Sort of a handoff. And it works great for the first year. Then I met Danny. Plain Danny. But he was different.

"With Danny, it wasn't all about him. He cared. Most of these guys won't even look you in the eye. Danny would really talk to me. If he saw me, he'd wave. No guy does that. I mean, it was still for money, he'd fuck my face, but he was decent about it. That first time I did him, shit, he said I looked beautiful sucking his dick. And he meant it! He was all concerned about me being OK, and 'Am I choking

42%
of men say they enjoy coming on their partner's face.

you?' Choking me? He had a dick like my thumb. But it was a beautiful dick, 'cause he was a beautiful guy. I gave him every trick I knew. Get him right to the point of blowing his wad, then pull him back. I did that for, like, a couple of hours. I'd mix it up with some kissing, a little light fucking, maybe some rimming, but I'd keep coming back to the blow job, because that's what men go out looking for, ladies. I'd never spend that much time with a guy, not for that kind of money anyway. But Danny was different. He's the only guy who ever once sent me a fucking 'thank you' card. It came on my birthday, but I don't think he knew that.

"I ran into Danny near the end of term. He introduced me to his fiancée as 'a good friend.' I ask you, who the hell does that? I saw her a couple of days later and bought her a latte. I sat her down and told her to take good care of Danny. And I told her how. I think she left a little stunned. But at the wedding she thanked me. Yeah, I got invited.

"So, like Judy, I've moved on to the Strip now too. And the main thing I've learned is it's not about sex, or money, or immorality, or any of that crap. It's about one thing: power. See, I've got talent, the john's got cash. Each of those is power. They get to sample my talent, but they hand over their cash to me. Who ends up with more power? They get nothing from me I don't take with me when I walk out the door. They get my time and a certain skill. But I'm a strong woman to the core. They never get my heart. Not anymore.

"And don't give me any bullshit about wasting my life. I got a bitchin' condo here in Vegas, I got over half a million in my IRA, I got real estate at Lake Havasu, and a part ownership in a cooking school, so get over it. Besides, I majored in philosophy. What else was I gonna do?"

What Have We Learned? Mimi tells us:

1. Most men can be pretty easy to please with a blow job.
2. Go into the blow job with a menu of things to do (see chapters 6 and 7), and be willing to improvise.

3. Whatever makes him jump—in a good way—do more of.

4. A person will do a hell of a lot more for a man who really treats them nicely and with care and respect.

5. A little dick can be a beautiful dick—and a turn-on.

6. A blow job doesn't have to be exclusively a blow job but a part of your sexual relations.

7. Men who don't get blow jobs go looking for blow jobs.

8. You can make a pretty good living on your knees.

9. Unless "Vegas whore" is an acceptable career choice for you, consider majoring in something you can actually use!

GETTING/GIVING THE BEST

Well, you read the dirty stories, you big perv, and hopefully learned a few things demonstrated in them. (Gee, porno with a point! Who knew?) The main thing to learn being that both giving and getting a blow job can be a very hot experience, one that can be incorporated into your lovemaking very successfully.

The thing that helped make the difference in these stories is that in each case there was care and attention given. And not just to the dick and the balls and the whatever but, much more importantly, to the *person,* whether giving the blow job or receiving it. You see, in addition to all the tricks, personal consideration and respect should never be overlooked. If you're on the receiving end, you owe it to the guy or gal swinging on your vine for the good time you're getting.

If you're the giver, you should demand it. Communicate, connect, and be aware of your own needs. How do you manage that? Are you shitting me? What's wrong with you, you fat-headed, stretched-out old cow? Sweet Satan, I don't know why we bother with you thought-free freaks.

Now, where were we? Oh, yes, respect. Respect and interest make a person feel spe-

50%
of men say that they don't receive enough oral sex.

cial. Attention and technique make him orgasm. Put the two together—along with the other things we learned from those naughty stories—and you have a very powerful and sexy force. And may the force be with you!

9
LOCATION, LOCATION, LOCATION

You've read all about techniques, things to do beyond the penis, dos and don'ts, positions, blah blah blah. So could it really be all that important *where* this delightfully disgusting deed transpires? Like everything else about sex, it depends on to whom you talk. For many people, there's nothing like a little touch of the unexpected or unorthodox to spice things up. It's an excellent way to keep your knob slobbing—or any other part of your love life—from getting into a rut. Depending on your tastes, you might enjoy your blow job someplace daring, outré, or dangerous.

Now, we're not suggesting that you should do something stupid that'll get you in trouble with community decency laws. No, no, no. Despite the fact that you would not be the first person to find blowing someone in jail a memorable experience, we believe most people would want to avoid that. We do not want our readers to have an unpleasant experience like that because (A) we care about you—really, we do—and (B) we don't want you suing our asses because you think we told you to get your face fucked under the traffic light at 1st and Main. Use your head! Er, the one on your shoulders, we mean.

So where should you go for your hummer? Perhaps you're not sure what would make a good place for sucking cock. Maybe it sounds like something that's too scary to even consider. That's understandable. That's also why we went to some considerable trouble to find fine examples that not only gently encourage, affirm, assure, and teach but will help you get your rocks off. Pay attention and you may notice that several of the same things come up again and again. There's a reason for that: They work.

GOING DOWN WHILE GOING UP

My girlfriend I were going to Japan on the red-eye. It was a light flight, so there were no other passengers sitting in our row all the way across the plane. We were in front of our section, right at the wall where the movie screen comes down. The plane had taxied for take-off and the captain had called for the flight attendants to take their positions or whatever. Basically, they were strapped in on the other side of the wall we were facing. That's when she pushed the armrest up and reached over. She yanked my button-fly jeans open, pulled my dick out, and went down on me. The engines surged, and we started down the runway with her leaning over me, sucking away. She stayed on it as we left the ground and started to climb. It was so unexpected and hot that I came just as we heard the flight attendants on the other side of the wall unbuckle their seat belts.

WHAT MADE THIS HOT:

1. Danger of getting caught.
2. Unexpected local.
3. Unexpected time.
4. Aggressive moves from the girlfriend.
5. Girlfriend took advantage of the situation.
6. It was sex with his partner. Yes, partners are hot. And you can tell his appreciation of the nerve of his girlfriend, something he will always carry with him in his "girlfriend is sexy" file!

EATING OUT

There were at least a dozen of us crammed into one of those large corner booths at a T.G.I. Friday's. We were celebrating Thom and Jim's imminent opening of a new gay club in Charlotte, N.C. Back in the pre-AIDS '70s, T.G.I. Friday's was just about the epitome of Charlotte night life, so any new club was cause for celebration. I was sitting next to Thom. He and Jim had hired themselves "escorts." Thom's escort, Roger, had given me some looks, but I figured they were purely professional. He was a few years younger than me; college-age; long, dark hair; green eyes. The conversation turned to techniques for the best blow jobs. The escorts, Roger and Clif, got into an argument over who was best. With a wink in my direction, Roger claimed he could make a man come inside of two minutes. Jim, who'd had several drinks by then, suggested a contest. The escorts were to slip under the table and give Thom and Jim oral sex. If Thom came first, Roger was the best; if Jim came first, Clif was.

The guys gathered around the table conspiratorially to hide what was going on. It was very exciting, decadent, and tinged with danger, which made the scene very hot. Someone said "Go!" and the escorts got down to business. I could feel Thom's legs pressing rhythmically against mine as Roger made good on his claim. Thom came first, pounding on the table, bouncing tableware, followed almost immediately by Jim, who dug his fingers into the friends on each side. The guys cheered. Clif came back up, but Roger didn't appear. Then I felt his hand on my crotch. I froze.

He pulled down my zipper and wrestled my hard dick out of my Jockey shorts. The guys could tell what was going on by the look on my face. When Roger's warm mouth slobbered down on my cock, I had to grab the side of the table. Good God, this guy was amazing! This was going to take no time at all. Everyone was absolutely silent, watching my twitching expression. All these men were watching me while another was blowing me under the table. All of them wanting me to come. And I couldn't hold it back. I felt the

65% of gay men say that they like the taste of semen.

gush starting and I bit my shoulder to keep from yelling in the restaurant. I lost my grip on the table and slid down in my seat a little. Then Roger's hand came up, grabbed my shirt, and pulled me the rest of the way under the table!

It was cramped and awkward. I crouched and turned to see Roger. His face was hot and wet. He put his hand behind my neck and pulled me to his lips. We kissed. Suddenly I realized he had my load in his mouth. He passed it to me. A wave of shock shot through me. I thought, *This is too sick.* Then I thought, *This is so hot!* And I kissed him even harder, passing it back and forth with a thrill of taboo while he beat off. Roger moaned, his dripping mouth still on mine, as he came all over my khakis. I would be wearing his jizz home. That was fine with me. After a couple of moments he caught his breath and we smiled at each other. We wriggled our way back up into our booth seats. Nobody up there had breathed. Somebody asked, "What happened down there?" Roger and I just grinned. I signaled to a waiter. "Could we get some napkins, please?"

WHAT MADE THIS HOT:
1. Danger of getting caught—twice!
2. Public place.
3. Very unexpected.
4. Lots of sexually aggressive moves.
5. Already outrageous situation made even more so.
6. Action didn't stop after the blow job.
7. A very talented blower. Never underestimate a professional!

YO HO, BLOW THE MAN DOWN

My divorce had just become final, and I was really depressed over it. My ex had left me for a younger woman; how much more typical could you get? My rich girlfriend decided I needed a lift, so she bought us a Caribbean cruise. So there we were in a ballroom dancing class off St. Croix when the captain dropped in. He said he loved dancing and was my partner for one dance. That afternoon I received a note in my cabin inviting me to dine at the captain's table. Well! We hit it off like there was nobody else at the table. He was so handsome, white hair and gray eyes. His hands were large and strong but refined. Manicured but no polish. And that uniform! He offered to give me a tour of the ship after dinner. I accepted, of course. I felt like such a VIP. Passengers wondered who I was, and

37% of men say that their partners rarely ask them what they like during oral sex.

the staff and crew snapped to when we entered anywhere. I saw everything from the engine room to the bridge. I even took the helm for a few minutes.

The next night was a dance, and he asked if he could escort me. I'm not a very good dancer, but he knew how to lead and made me look and feel like I was the most graceful dancer on the floor. We managed to spend time together every day of the cruise, laughing and never running out of conversation. On the last night he asked if I'd like a tour of the ship. I reminded him we had done that days ago. He kissed my hand and said, "Yes, but I don't believe you saw the captain's quarters."

I couldn't believe it. He must pull this every cruise. Find a single woman and sweep her off her feet with the whole captain thing. And you know what? I decided I didn't care. In five days he made me feel more special than the last five years I spent with Alan. So we made love in the captain's quarters. Maybe it was because I knew I'd never see him again or because I hadn't had sexual contact with a man in over a year, but I felt so free, I was finally able to enjoy giving a man oral sex. I made him wear a condom, which he was very gracious about, but I'm pleased to say I was not only successful, but I was so excited that when he climaxed, I did too. When he caught his breath, he pulled me up on the bed to give me oral pleasure. When my ex was done, he wanted to see what was on TV. This man, though, wanted to make sure I was satisfied. And oh, was I ever.

I couldn't believe it, but after some champagne he was ready to go at it again! At his age! I tell you, there must be something about all that salt air.

WHAT MADE THIS HOT:

1. She was ready, both emotionally and sexually.
2. She had been made to feel special by his show of respect, special treatment, and romance.
3. He respected her wishes.
4. He reciprocated.
5. He reciprocated. No, that's not a typo, we want to make sure you BJ receivers really get that, OK?
6. And it didn't hurt he was ready to go again.

GALLEY SLAVE

I'm 6 foot 8, so I tend to stand out. On top of that, I was wearing red leather, head to toe. I was going from Palm Springs to San Francisco for Castro Street Fair. When I got on the little United shuttle, I had to duck. The flight attendant said, "You tall boys always have trouble." He was clearly flirting with me, and every time he passed we exchanged looks. After we took off, I looked down the aisle to the back of the plane where the tiny galley and bathroom were. I got up and went back there.

"Close quarters, huh?" he said as I slipped past him, making no attempt to create more room for me to pass. Once in the bathroom, I took my pants down and opened the folding bathroom door a crack. He was bending down, stowing glassware next to the bathroom. He saw me standing there with a hard-on. He raised an eyebrow. I opened the door wider.

"Suck it," I said. He looked up the aisle to make sure no one was coming, then whispered, "Yes, sir." Making it look like he was stowing the glasses, he took my dick in his mouth each time he leaned forward to put one away. If anyone had come back, we would have been caught. It was so dangerous that it only took me a few dozen "glasses" to come. He took it all too. I guess he couldn't afford to get any on the uniform!

WHAT MADE THIS HOT:

1. Unexpected.
2. Overt, aggressive sexuality from both parties.
3. Danger of getting caught.
4. Public location.

"DRIVE," HE SAID

It was my birthday. My fiancée thought he'd really go out of his way to make this day special for me. The evening entailed a helicopter tour of the city, and then off to one of the hottest restaurants in town, ending with a stay in a luxury hotel room. The best part was that he also had us being charioted by a limousine all night. Right from the start I was feeling extremely wanton by the sheer effort he went through for me. On the way to the restaurant we were making out and partaking in some heavy petting in the back of the limo. (Love those partitions!)

We were about 10 minutes from the restaurant when it occurred to me. Yes, I wanted to give him something to say thank you, but it was more than that. I happen to love giving my boyfriend head. Not only does it turn me on, but it gives me a great sense of accomplishment making him come. Maybe it's a control thing. I love to see how fast I can make him come by giving him head. At first he resisted because we were so close to the restaurant, but then he surrendered. Of course, once I've already pulled him out of his pants, what is he going to say, "no"? The time restraint only added more to the thrill— as we got closer he got more anxious and I got more excited. While our car was in line in front of the valet, with only three cars ahead of us, he came. With no evidence left and with not a moment to spare, the door opened and we went on with our perfect evening, all the while smirking with what we got away with!

WHAT MADE THIS HOT:

1. It was a pleasure for her to do this.

2. She knows and claims her power in giving her boyfriend blow jobs.
3. She had been made to feel special.
4. It was unexpected.
5. She initiated the blow job.
6. Unusual location for them.
7. The excitement of taking advantage of a very limited opportunity.

LET'S ALL GO TO THE LOBBY

I'd been dating Josh, and he just wasn't doing it for me. I guess I was just looking for an excuse to break up. Anyway, we went to a multiplex to see some horror movie. I remember thinking this movie was only marginally better than my non-relationship. Anyway, when it was over we went to the men's room, which was right next to some PG-rated family movie that was also letting out, and all those people where in there too, so it was crowded. My soon-to-be-ex took his piss and left. I took his urinal. Next to me, on the end of the wall, there was this 18-year-old blond surfer dude. He was so hot and he was showing me this huge hard-on in this busy bathroom full of fathers and sons. A man came out of the bathroom stall near where we were. The surfer went over to it and entered. Then he turned and stared at me, holding the door open. With all those people there, I walked right over and shut the door. He went down on me. God, he was gorgeous, and just knowing that everyone who saw us knew exactly what was going on in that stall was a major kick. The surfer guy wasn't being particularly quiet, either, so neither was I. It took no time at all for me to come all over his face. I licked most of it off while he beat off, shooting all over my shirt. Anyway, we wiped off, more or less, then opened the door and walked out together—just as Josh came back in looking for me! He saw us come out of the stall and started calling me every slut name in the

48% of people say that they'd give better head if their man would say what he wants.

book. Whew, what a scene. I think a lot of dads had a lot to explain to their kids that day!

WHAT MADE THIS HOT:

1. Already emotionally charged from film and date.
2. Ballsy display of sexuality.
3. Unexpected.
4. Daring offer.
5. Public place.
6. Disregard for others knowing what was going on.

MAKING BEAUTIFUL MUSIC TOGETHER

My boyfriend proposed to me on July 3, so I was very happy. The next day was July 4, and he made it wonderful for me. Breakfast in bed, the big announcement at the family barbecue, showing everybody the ring, it was great. That night we went to the esplanade to hear the Boston Pops perform. If you don't know Boston, it's outdoors by the water—this long, beautiful park where they perform and there's boats out on the Charles River. They do this big concert and everybody comes, big mobs of people all having a great time, and it's wonderful. Near the end of the concert it's getting dark. We're over kinda by some bushes on our blanket, kissing and making out. I'm feeling so great 'cause this man who treats me like I'm a princess is gonna be my husband and he loves me so much. They start playing the 1812 Overture, and I'm so happy I snuggle up with my head in his lap. And I can tell he's excited, you know what I'm saying? It's pretty good and dark now and the bushes are kinda hiding us, so I'm rubbing my head against him. You know. Then, the music gets to the big, loud part, when all of a sudden they start setting off the fireworks. That's when I decide to go for it. I rolled over and unzipped his pants. The fireworks are lighting up the park, but everybody was looking up while I was going down. It's so exciting being right out in the open like this—well, near the bushes, but not really. I can tell he's about ready because he grinds his teeth and kinda moans with his mouth closed. You know, "mmmm."

And the cannons start going off with the music and that does it. It happens, and I thought he was gonna pass out or something. I got the blanket over him so he doesn't have to put it away right away and we can just lay there. And they start ringing the bells at the end—Christ, every church bell in Boston it seemed was ringing. And you know what? He was crying. Not sad crying but happy. And then I cried because I was so happy too. I will always remember that. We were both so happy. And we had gotten away with murder there in the park too.

WHAT MADE THIS HOT:

1. Emotionally charged event.
2. She was feeling very special.
3. Beautiful location.
4. Public space.
5. Danger of being seen.
6. Music and visuals can help.
7. They both cried for joy afterward. *That's* what great sex can do!

BARELY LEGAL LOVIN'

Oral sex is what I love best. I love giving head and I'm really good. I grew up in Cincinnati. A preacher's kid. I knew I was gay from the time I was 10. By the time I was 14, I'd already had oral sex with a few of my friends. When I was 18, I got a computer when I went to college, and a whole new world opened up! I met so many people. But the hottest place I ever gave head…well, let me set it up.

I'm online, looking for sex. I'm supposed to be studying for a test, but I mean, chemistry? When I could be sucking dick? Anyway, I meet this guy and we go into a private chat room. He's a cop, he's 27, and he wants me to blow him. So I sneak out the window and walk three blocks over. I'm standing on the corner and he pulls up in his cruiser in uniform. He opens the door. He was very hot. Big, you know? We drive to this dirt road you can hardly see and pull in so no one sees the police car from the road. He turns the lights off except for this little one on the dash. He's got the police radio turned down, but I can still hear it sputter and crackle with cop talk. That and the smell of the car just made it even hotter. He opened his pants and I went to work. He was ready to pop, but I like a good hard dick too much to let it go, so I slow down. Make him wait. I sucked off this big-ass cop in his police car for almost an hour before I let him come. And when he did, he was a gusher. He must have liked it, because we did it about twice a month for over two years. Sometimes he'd handcuff me. Even then I never missed a drop.

WHAT MADE THIS HOT:

1. He took matters into his own hands and went looking for someone who wanted it.

2. A generally "off limits" location in the squad car.

3. Visuals (car and uniform), sounds (cop radio), and smells (car, gun, etc.) added.

4. He was blowing a fucking *cop*, for chrissakes!

5. He took his time and had repeat business.

6. Props (handcuffs) were introduced.

SIX PEOPLE WHO REALLY SUCK

Whew, OK, that's enough steamy stories for now. We're going to bring the room down a bit with a group of people who actually keep their clothes on. We wanted to find out where ordinary people like to give and/or get their blow jobs. We gathered six everyday folks around a tape recorder and asked for their views on where they like to lick. Those people were:

KELLIE: 33, straight, married 12 years, two children, cashier.

TIM: 28, straight, divorced, no children, car salesman.

SUE: 41, straight, divorced, no children, currently has a boyfriend of three years, legal secretary.

ANTHONY: 21, gay, single, veterinarian's assistant.

CINDY: 24, straight, married two years, high school teacher.

GEORGE: 45, gay, divorced, one grown child, currently in a seven-year relationship, loan officer.

INSTINCT: Let's start off by describing our favorite places for giving or receiving blow jobs. Kellie, why don't you lead us off?

KELLIE: Well, it may not be imaginative, but I like the bedroom because it's quiet, it has privacy, and I can keep the kids out.

ANTHONY: Ew, kids? Kids are a total wood kill.

KELLIE: Trust me, you get used to 'em and you can tune 'em out. Anyway, it's intimate and familiar and comfortable. I tell you, you can't beat the bedroom.

TIM: A bedroom works. Even better is a strange bedroom.

CINDY: One time we were visiting my husband's parents and we did the, you know, oral thing in his parents' bedroom. He really got off on it.

TIM: OK, that's a little too strange.

ANTHONY: What about the privacy?

CINDY: Oh, they took the kids to a movie, so we were safe.

SUE: I love it best when it's really dangerous. Not like you're gonna get killed but like you could get caught. I was dating this guy who ran a car rental agency, one of these hole-in-the-wall satellite offices. Basically just him, the counter, and the cars out back. I just dropped by to say hi and, well, I unzipped his pants, took it out, and started blowing him. Normally, nobody ever comes in, but that night a couple comes in to rent a car. There was plenty of room under the counter, so I just shifted over there and kept at it. Zack's trying to be cool about it, but he's fumbling the deal, stammering—eventually he just gave 'em a bunch of keys and told 'em to go pick whichever one they liked just to get rid of them.

KELLIE: I still love the bedroom, because it's made for noise and positions and everything else you want to put into it.

SUE: But that's so safe.

KELLIE: Yeah, which is why you can let loose any way you want. Why would I want to do something risky?

SUE: For the thrill!

KELLIE: I don't need a thrill, I have kids.

TIM: I like the dangerous-like-you-could-get-killed thing.

INSTINCT: Explain what you mean, Tim.

TIM: To me, there's nothing hotter than getting blown while driving. The speed and the action are totally hot. And the concentration just to keep from going off the road until you do come, it's awesome.

KELLIE: It's reckless!

TIM: I like it. And man, do I come!

KELLIE: Here's my number. Call me when you're going out for a drive so I'll know to stay home.

TIM: Yeah, in your safe little bedroom.

KELLIE: Fuck you, I hope you and your bimbo hit a major pothole.

INSTINCT: Ouch! OK, OK, let's settle down. What about sex in public?

CINDY AND ANTHONY: Yes!

INSTINCT: That's what we like, enthusiasm. All right, Cindy, ladies first.

CINDY: Well, I'm with Sue on this one. I love starting something in the mall or a restaurant or something. It totally freaks my husband out. I mean, I gotta get past his embarrassment sometimes, but I think he kinda looks forward to it. It certainly keeps him on his toes, 'cause he never knows if I'm gonna start something or where I might do it. He never complains, though, once I start, you know…

ANTHONY: It's called sucking.

CINDY: Yeah. I wish it had a nicer name.

ANTHONY: Like face-fucking?

CINDY: [*Laughing*] Ew, stop!

KELLIE: Back up, here. OK, you're at the restaurant: Exactly what do you mean "you start something"?

CINDY: You know, maybe I'll drop my fork and lean under the table and grab a quick gnawing at his crotch while I'm down there. Then maybe a spoon or my napkin.

KELLIE: And this doesn't attract attention?

CINDY: That's kinda the fun. It makes Tom embarrassed but excited. I think he gets off on knowing other people know what's going on too.

KELLIE: OK, what next?

CINDY: Well, I'll unzip him and start handling it.

TIM: OK, this has gotta be a decent restaurant, one with tablecloths, right?

CINDY: Well, yeah. I mean, duh. It's at a restaurant I know too, so I know where I'm going. So no, I wouldn't try this at Sizzler.

KELLIE: This is nuts. Then what?

CINDY: Then I'll get up and tell him to meet me in, like, the coat room if it's not being used, or the ladies' room if it's a one-seater, or something. Don't look at me that way—I told you, it's a place I know where I'm going.

KELLIE: You cased the joint?

CINDY: In a way. Same thing at the mall. Get him started by groping him a few times in the men's department—

ANTHONY: What is that, a euphemism?

CINDY: Huh?

ANTHONY: Never mind.

CINDY: Then I just lead him to a deserted corridor behind a store or something and get on my knees and I, you know…

ANTHONY: Suck him! You suck his cock, honey.

GEORGE: That so pisses me off.

CINDY: Why?

GEORGE: Because if anyone comes down that corridor and sees you blowing your husband, they just turn around and walk away. If it was me blowing him, they'd call security and arrest us.

SUE: That's what you get for blowing her husband.

GEORGE: You know what I mean. And hers wouldn't be the first married man I've sucked. Or been sucked by.

CINDY: Well, I can't help that. I'm just telling you about how doing it at the mall or in public can be exciting.

TIM: More like slutty. If some woman tried that with me in a mall, I'd dump her right there.

SUE: Oh, please, you get a man hard and he'd do it on a table in the food court.

INSTINCT: Anthony, you also liked the public side of blow jobs. Tell us why.

ANTHONY: It's a power thing. If I'm getting a blow job, I want people to see it. I want people watching me get my dick sucked, that this man would want to suck my cock. I love it even more when they join in or I can look around and see them getting off on watching me. The energy goes around the room, you can smell the sweat, hear people coming.

TIM: Wow. I'm going to the wrong parties.

GEORGE: Yeah, straight ones.

ANTHONY: I'll invite you, Tom.

TIM: Tim. Pass.

ANTHONY: Actually, you don't even have to be invited. It's a sex club.

TIM: What's that?

GEORGE: It's one of the advantages of being gay. We're men, we're horny—

KELLIE: Redundant!

GEORGE: Granted. So we invented a place to go to get off. Suck and fuck and go on your way.

TIM: Oh, my God! This goes on?

SUE: At least he's not endangering oncoming traffic.

TIM: Do you think you could let that go already?

INSTINCT: What about having people watch you give a blow job?

ANTHONY: Oh, yeah! It's all about the power. Knowing people are watching me give this guy so much pleasure they wish it was them. Looking up and seeing them watching me while they stroke their dicks in rhythm to how I'm sucking, pretending their hand is my mouth. Hoping they can be next. It's great both ways.

GEORGE: Ever thought about getting it both ways, Tim? [*The women laugh*]

ANTHONY: A sex club or a bathhouse is kind of like Kellie's bedroom.

KELLIE: What?

ANTHONY: Sorry, I don't mean it like that. It's like having a place you can feel comfortable about letting loose. It's a private club, no one's going to arrest you, that's what it's for.

KELLIE: It's not that private. Anyone can walk in and, well, do whatever.

ANTHONY: If you're lucky.

KELLIE: Call me old-fashioned, but I like the one-on-one in private. I like being able to concentrate on what I'm doing.

TIM: Hear, hear.

KELLIE: And I sure don't want to worry about competition. If I'm going to be giving him oral sex, I want his undivided attention.

INSTINCT: We haven't heard from you, George. Where is your favorite place?

GEORGE: Well, my therapist and I are working on my favorite places. It used to be public rest rooms.

GROUP: Eww!

GEORGE: Thanks for being nonjudgmental and understanding.

INSTINCT: We apologize for the group, George. Why was that a turn-on for you?

GEORGE: For a lot of the same reasons you, you, you, and you gave. [*Pointing to Sue, Anthony, Tim, and Cindy*] It was exciting. The danger of it was a big factor because at any time I could have been caught and we'd have been arrested. Maybe not we-could-get-killed danger but enough to make it pretty intense if we were. Caught, I mean.

SUE: But you're a good-looking man; you didn't have to do that.

GEORGE: Thanks, lady, but I did have to. For the thrill and the danger. And the degradation. And the addiction. Like you would understand.

SUE: You know, it's possible you're not the only one in recovery here.

GEORGE: Great, let's get together, drink coffee, and chain-smoke.

INSTINCT: OK, Bitter Betty, you said your favorite place used to be rest rooms. What are they now?

GEORGE: That's not so easy to say. I mean, while I don't do the tea-rooms anymore, I still really like inappropriate places.

ANTHONY: I'm confused, what's "inappropriate places" mean?

GEORGE: For me, it means malls, restaurants, and places like rent-a-car offices, which are all fine and good for you, but my ass can get arrested for that. So for the time being, my blow job place of choice is my house, his house, or a hotel.

INSTINCT: Aren't you in a relationship, George?

GEORGE: [*Sighs*] I'm seeing a cop.

TIM: Holy shit.

GEORGE: And he's not out. He's very closeted. If I go to his house, I have to drive into the garage. He gave me a remote so I can close it before I get out so no one will see me.

SUE: Oh, that's healthy.

GEORGE: You wanna know about inappropriate places? How about the holding room at the police station? It was totally stupid—anyone could walk in. I mean, this is a police station, for God's sake. There's cops all over the place and we're blowing each other in the fucking pokey room.

ANTHONY: OK, I want to be supportive here, but your story's giving me a chubby.

GEORGE: That was the problem, that it was so damn hot. But it was like screaming to get caught. His career would be ruined, I'd be arrested, it's a small town, we'd both have to move. So we have an agreement. Only in his house or my house. Or a hotel out of town. And at his house, he'll only do it in the bedroom. Ugh, it's very stressful.

KELLIE: But that's OK. You can have a lot of fun in the bedroom. I tell you, those are the best. I love the bedroom.

TIM: What's a tearoom?

ANTHONY: It ain't tea you drink. It's "T" as in "toilet."

TIM: My God, you guys do it everywhere. Do you ever stop having sex?

ANTHONY: Well, we're taking time out to talk with you.

GEORGE: And that's an offensive gay stereotype. I'm not getting on a high horse here. I'm just saying.

TAKING THE PLUNGE

Whether you are thinking of varying your routine, spicing up your love life, or just needing a change of scenery, below are some suggestions you may wish to consider. While we don't pretend this is an exhaustive or complete list, it should be enough to get you started on a place or two to try, or spark some ideas of your own.

FUN PLACES TO FUCK FACES:
First off, every room in the house.
Including the basement.
Including the attic (watch out for that insulation!)
Someone else's house.
The backyard.
A junkyard.
Your garage.
Your mechanic's garage.
In the great outdoors.
Behind a billboard.
In the department store dressing room.
In a closet at a party.
On the roof.
At the beach.
At the movies.
At the theater.
Opera.
Ballet.
Symphony.
Recital.
In the bushes.
While he's trying to talk on the phone.
Church or temple.
School.

TIM: Oh, give me a break with the stereotypes. I know how bad I want a blow job, or any sex, for that matter. Men—any man—wants sex, period, end of story. That's why you're all over each other, you can do that. But women, women gotta have a reason. And that's why getting any is so damn hard. If women just wanted sex the way men do—

SUE: Everyone would be dicks.

INSTINCT: Let's get back to blow jobs. Can we go around the table for any final thoughts? Start with Cindy.

CINDY: Well, I like giving blow jobs, but then I like pretty much everything. Of course, we've only been married two years, so who knows? I mean, I hear it gets dull after a while, so I don't want that. I want to keep learning new things and trying it different places so we don't get into, like, a rut or something.

KELLIE: Well, honey, it will get boring. But you'll get over it. It comes and goes, but if you really love him, it'll be enough. Life's not all about sex. I guess I'd have to say there's really something to be said for tried-and-true. A blow job at home is just part of our sex life.

CINDY: Does he, you know, reciprocate?

KELLIE: Oh, yeah. Or there'd be no blow job at home! I'm just kidding, he's a good man. Um, that's it for me.

ANTHONY: My turn? Blow jobs, two thumbs up! 'Course, I'd say that about fucking, rimming, dildos, hand jobs, and jerking off.

TIM: Jesus, anything else?

ANTHONY: Um, yeah, the other night I was just rubbing myself all over this guy covered with lube and we both came—what would you call that?

SUE: Too much information.

ANTHONY: Oh. Well, then I'm done. Um, Tom?

TIM: Tim. And from what I've learned today, all I can say is, I wish I could be one of you guys, only with women.

GEORGE: A crossover homo?

TIM: I want the sex you get, only with their body parts.

ANTHONY: You know, the mouth is the same on a man or a woman, if you'd like to try it, Tom.

TIM: It's Tim!

At the drive-in.
At the drive-through (c'mon, that's semi-parked).
Gym.
Spa.
Hotel.
Someone else's hotel room!
Cabana.
Lifeguard station.
Swimming pool.
Motor pool.
Country club.
Officer's club.
Inside a tank.
Helicopter.
In a balloon.
Backstage.
Center stage.
In the backseat of the bus.
The bus station.
A police station.
Roller rink.
Laundromat.
Tent.
Treehouse.
A bar.
A back room.
In the shed.
In the alley.
Parking lot.
Museum.
Rodeo.
Summer camp.
Grocery. (It can be done!)
Bookstore.
Rock concert.
The House.
The Senate.
The Oval Office.
Under a Supreme Court justice's robe.
Park ranger lodge.

129

Cabin in the woods.
Ball game.
Hospital.
Airport.
Cockpit. (While on autopilot, please!)
Train station.
Construction site.
Under a bridge, with all those cars going by overhead.
Dark rides at theme parks. (Can you say, "Haunted Mansion"?)
The circus. (Big clown shoes = big clown dick!)
In a trailer.
Ski lodge.
Library. (Shhh!)
The roof.
Fire escape.
Firehouse.
Courthouse.
Boathouse.
An abandoned factory.
A busy factory.
A cave or grotto.
At your office desk.
On the freaking boardroom table!
Would you do it at a party?
I'd blow a guy on a tractor.
Or better yet, in a cornfield.
Would you blow me on a boat?
In a castle with a moat?
A barn, a hayloft, or a stable?
Anywhere I'm fucking able!
I would blow you on a train.
I would blow you in the rain.
I would blow you in a chair.
I would blow you anywhere.
I would blow you, Sam I am.
Sure, I would suck your dick, hot damn!

ANTHONY: I know.

TIM: Asshole.

ANTHONY: Come to think of it, that's the same too.

INSTINCT: But it's a different book, Anthony. Anything else, Tim?

TIM: No. Just bring on the blow jobs, ladies!

SUE: Tell you what, Tim, why don't you go to your car and wait for me? [*Group laughs*] I want to say something about what Cindy said. I can't speak for other women, but I'm the oldest woman here, and sex has never been boring to me. Sometimes my partner has been boring, which is something totally different.

CINDY: What did you do?

SUE: You work with what you have. If it doesn't improve and there's nothing else, move on.

GEORGE: Is it my turn? Sorry. Uh, well, the main thing I got out of this is I've got a lot of sorting out to do. But as for blow jobs, well, I love giving them. I'm very good. Years of practice and all that. I actually like giving them better than getting them. Same with being fucked.

ANTHONY: Oh, my God, your cop is a top! The chubby is so coming back.

GEORGE: I'll have Troy call you.

ANTHONY: Hot closeted cop love! You into three-ways?

GEORGE: You're asking a guy who used to cruise rest stops on the interstate?

ANTHONY: All right! Tell your friend to wear his uniform, and I swallow, so he won't have to dry-clean.

TIM: Gross! Excuse me, are we done here?

GEORGE: [*Laughs*] Sorry. Um, so I'm very pro–blow job. The where of it, though, is going to remain a major issue for me, for us, for a while. And I'll work on getting him to let me blow him someplace new but not inappropriate.

INSTINCT: Best of luck to you, George. And on behalf of sexual people everywhere, thank you for sharing your stories, intimate secrets, and personal lives with us.

TAKING THE PLUNGE

It is our hope that we've convinced you to at least entertain the idea of being adventurous in your choice of location. If it's not something you want to do right away, simply fold the corner of this page over and move on. When you decide to give it a go, all these ideas will be right here waiting for you.

10
LET'S FINISH THIS OFF

Hey, whaddaya know? All that stuff we talked about in the introduction came to pass. We've told you how to embrace and enjoy giving your blow job. You've learned all about the dick and balls and how they work so you won't be afraid of them. We went over the importance of communicating with your partner and have given you things to consider before you have sex of any kind with anyone. There was a big ol' chapter on actual techniques for what to do with Señor Snake, including an entire separate chapter on deep-throating. You got tips on how to make it special and where to make it happen, not to mention some pretty decent porno along the way just for titillation. We gave you facts and figures in the corners and sidebars. Hell, we even drew pictures for you. Now it's your turn to get out there and get some lips-on experience under your belt. Or under his. Because when it comes to something as complex as human sexuality, there's stuff you just can't learn without rolling up your sleeves and getting on your knees and doing the deed.

You see, this book was never meant to be the be-all and end-all instruction book for blow jobs. There is just too much wonderful variation in personalities, preferences, and penises for that. We knew that all we could hope to do was four things: (1) describe the basics, (2) allay some fears, (3) give you enough examples of the variety of things you can do so you would feel capable and willing to explore further on your own, and (4) tell some dirty stories to entertain and inspire you. And we wanted to do all that in a way that was refreshingly judgment-free, promoted a sex-positive attitude, and had a sense of humor and adventure. So if you didn't like it, get fucked.

No, we mean that. If, after all this, you have decided that cock sucking is not for you, go back to the regular fucking you were doing and enjoy the hell out of that. Doomed as you may be to mere missionary merging, if that's your pathology, who are we to make fun of freaks like you? We sincerely want you to get off on whatever sex you're having. We also want you to take dirty Polaroids of it and send them in to us too. Really, after all our work, it's the least you could do.

But you probably won't even do that. Damn, if you're still all squeamish about gettin' jiggy with his johnson, you could at least think of us, you little ingrate. Yeah, us. We worked our knees off for this miserable book. Doesn't that count for anything in your selfish little world? We stole many hours from our day jobs to bring you the finest in fellatio, teach you top-job knob slobbing, and present paragons of peter polishing, all in an effort to transform you into a crack cocksucker and make your hummers humdingers. We endured countless excruciating orgasms and sacrificed spazillions of sperm in supremely selfless acts to bring you this book. How could you let all that hard-won information, hard work, and hard dick go to waste? Please, please reconsider. Go back and flip though this book to try to find one reason for honing his bone. Really. That's all we ask. Well, that, and that you buy many, many copies of this book for each of your friends. They make excellent gifts. (The books, not your friends.)

Don't you see that by munching on his man meat, you're making his personal world just terrific? He's bound to want to rock your world by doing something equally pleasurable for you. Who knows what kind of cumulative effect that'll have? And just think, if all the folks who have read this book and taken it to heart are out there giving quality blow jobs and making their delighted partners want to do them in return, the happiness quotient for the planet has gotta be going way up. Plus, the more happy people there are, the more they'll affect those around them in positive ways from an ever-widening ripple effect that goes on and on and on! Wow, it's so "Circle of Life," only with a hard-on!

So for those of you who have decided to try making the blow job your main lovemaking event from time to time, we can't tell you how happy that makes us. If you've already been smoking dick for a while and have learned a few things that'll help you improve your game, then we can't wait to drop our pants and meet you. Send us a postcard, we'll be there! The bad news is that we'll be grading you. The good news is that neatness doesn't count.

Going over the main points one last time:
1. Everyone is different—respect and enjoy that.
2. If either of you don't like something, don't do it.
3. Once you decide not to do that, *do something else.*
4. Mix and match.
5. Explore on your own.
6. Enjoy it, damn it, or nobody will enjoy it.

Got that? Good, because this is a pop quiz! And, yes, it's an oral exam. Get out there and suck somebody! Or, as Queen Elizabeth said when she knighted Elton John: "On your knees, bitch!"